THE ARRANGEMENT

AMITY MALCOM

I0693945

This is a work of fiction. Names, characters, places, and incidents either are the product of the author's imagination or are used fictitiously. Any resemblance to actual persons, living or dead, events, or locales is entirely coincidental.

Copyright © 2022 by Amity Malcom

All rights reserved. No part of this book may be reproduced or used in any manner without written permission of the copyright owner except for the use of quotations in a book review.

To every woman who has lost her way only to find their true self in an unlikely place.

This one's for you.

Prologue

MYA FLUNG the door to Winston's Flowers open, a small bell signaling her entrance to the Upper East Side florist shop. Sashaying across the small store, a binder tucked under the arm of her classic Burberry trench, she stopped in front of the check-out counter, an audible sigh of irritation escaping her lips when no one was immediately there to welcome her.

She glanced at her watch-10:37 A.M.-before hastily tapping the silver call bell that sat on the counter several times.

A two-way door she hadn't noticed when she first entered the shop opened to her right, and a young girl cheerfully approached.

"Ma'am, welcome to Winston's Flowers! What can I do for you?"

Mya looked the woman over. The jeans she wore were faded and frayed, there was a small hole near the collar of her shirt, and the apron she had tightly tied around herself was dotted with stains of various sizes. The smile across the bottom half of her face was so large that it was almost comical.

"Hello, April," Mya said with a steely voice while looking at the name tag crookedly perched on the girl's apron. "I have an appointment with a Lucas Gentry."

The girl's smile didn't falter. "Sure, just a second," she chirped before scampering to the back room.

The instant the girl disappeared, Mya took in the shop. Flowers of every color and size were displayed in galvanized steel containers on floating shelves. There was a small selection of cards available for purchase as well as several stuffed animals and assorted candies. The scent of the floral arrangements hung heavy in the air, making Mya slightly nauseous.

She knew this was *the* place for wedding flowers and had seen many impressive articles chronicling large and expensive weddings that had used Winston's. Mya had even attended some of those weddings in person, so when it came to her own wedding, there was no doubt she wanted to follow in the footsteps of New York City's high society before her, even if she wasn't exactly excited about planning her wedding. However, looking around the small shop with its stuffed animals and latex balloons, she began to think she was in the wrong place.

A frown marred her face as she glanced at her watch once again-10:46 A.M. Lucas was officially late for their appointment, and Mya despised running behind almost as much as she hated the chilly November air she had to put up with on the short walk to the shop.

An interior designer at one of the largest design firms in New York City, Mya adhered to a strict sched-ule. She drank the same smoothie for breakfast every day except Sunday, went to the same spin class three times each week, kept herself meticulously groomed, always arrived at meetings early, and was the last to leave the office each night. She worked her way to the top, starting at her company as an intern while still in college. Mya knew her success was due to her drive and determination and was not about to become lax just because she was at the top of the proverbial food chain.

"Ahem." A deep voice came from behind Mya, causing her to jump. She turned towards the sound, her blunt, chin-length, black bob swaying with her movement.

"I'm so sorry. I didn't mean to startle you," the

man said. Outstretching his hand to Mya, he continued. "Lucas Gentry. I believe we have an appointment."

The man looked slightly disheveled, a messy mop of black hair atop his head. Piercing steel-blue eyes stared at Mya while a thick beard framed his slightly imperfect smile. A red and black plaid button-up stretched across a broad chest, suede patches over the elbows. He wore black jeans and Converse sneakers and looked nothing like Mya believed a well-respected business owner should appear.

Not taking his hand, Mya silently scoffed, thinking he looked more suited to the woods than the urban jungle of New York City. All he needed was an ax and some boots and he would be the perfect lumberjack.

"Mr. Gentry, I'm on a tight schedule, and you are running late for our meeting. Is now not an opportune time? Would you prefer I reschedule or take my business elsewhere?"

Dumbfounded, Lucas stared back at the beautiful woman before him, her perfectly sculpted brows pressed into a deep line. "I assure you, Ms-," he paused, suddenly aware that he did not know her last name.

"Monroe," she clipped.

"Ms. Monroe, I assure you there is nothing I would

rather be doing than helping you to plan the wedding you have always been dreaming of."

She rolled her eyes, an exacerbated sigh coming deep from her lungs while she pushed her binder into his hands. "I'm *not* that kind of woman, Mr. Gentry."

He cut her off before she could continue. "Please, call me Lucas."

"Mr. Gentry," she continued, ignoring his request as a sly smile crept across his lips, "I am the best at what I do, and while I do not quite believe it, you are apparently the best at what you do. Can we move forward with this meeting? I have a very busy day ahead of me."

Lucas flipped open the binder, fingering through the pages of wedding plans. Table linens, bridesmaid dresses, and flower arrangements dotted the pages. He closed the binder, tucking it beneath his arm before gesturing to the door that led to the rear of the shop. "Follow me, Ms. Monroe."

The workroom of the shop was almost twice the size of the sales floor. Coolers lined two walls, over-stuffed with long stems of flowers. Rows of shelves held vases and urns in various colors and sizes. Ribbon and twine hung on a long bar over an industrial sink, and several bouquets of flowers were hanging upside down in front of a window in what looked like an attempt to dry them.

Lucas loved what he did for a living-loved bringing joy to other people through his stunning floral displays-and while he was fine with occasionally working the sales floor, this back room was like an extension of his home. Here, he turned ordinary flowers into works of art. He was big and burly and didn't much care for people, but when he stepped through the doors of Winston's each day, he turned into a completely different man.

Lucas flipped open the binder once again, placing it on a large worktable that stood in the middle of the room. He took a seat on a stool and gestured to the one adjacent to his. She continued to stand.

"I can see you definitely have a vision for your day." He studied a picture of a large arrangement-ranunculus, peonies, and lisianthus spilled from atop a thin, tall stand. Eucalyptus and pampas grass were interspersed along with smaller flowers and greenery. "Classic with a touch of bohemian."

"Mr. Gentry..." Mya started.

He smiled, not deterred by her icy demeanor. "Please, call me Lucas."

She huffed before continuing. "Mr. Gentry, I am sure most women who come in here are ecstatic about planning their wedding, but I assure you, I am just looking forward to the day being over with. Can you make something like those pictures or not?"

He laughed, the sound echoing through the room. Mya returned his laugh with an ice-cold gaze. "Well, Ms. Monroe, seeing as how those are pictures of my work," he pointed to a few photos in the binder, "I'd say I should be able to accommodate your request for your wedding with no problem."

Lucas shuffled a few papers around before continuing. "July 17th?"

A curt nod was Mya's only response.

His eyes widened as he continued reading over the forms she had filled out online. "No budget, seven hundred guests, Ceremony at St. Patrick's Cathedral, and Plaza Hotel reception. That is quite possibly the most quintessential dream New York City wedding if I've ever seen one. And your fiancé is okay with what you have chosen? Normally, I see both halves of a couple when doing these things."

Mya's eyes narrowed on Lucas. "Not that it is any of your business, Mr. Gentry. But if you must know, my fiance is the one who has designed the wedding to *his* specifications. He is currently traveling, as he does often, leaving me to handle the details without him."

"I see," Lucas responded, his eyes returning to the paperwork.

An exasperated snort escaped Mya's mouth. "You see?" she continued, growing louder. "You *see*? No, Mr. Gentry, I don't think you do see."

His hands flew up in a sign of surrender, but Mya kept going. "I'm here because that is what my fiancé wants. I'm only having this *wedding*," she said the word with so much vitriol that it dripped from her lips, "because that is what my fiancé wants, what our families want."

She stopped, her chest heaving with anger.

"And what about you, Ms. Monroe?"

Her eyes met his for the first time since her tirade started. "What do you mean, what about me?"

"What do you want, Ms. Monroe?"

Mya seemed to consider his words, a pregnant pause in their conversation, before answering almost sullenly, "Honestly, I don't think anyone has asked me that once since Dave proposed."

"Well," Lucas started, running a hand through his unruly hair, "maybe it's time you ask yourself that question."

She contemplated what he said for only the briefest of moments before the ice in her eyes returned. "There isn't time for questions, Mr. Gentry. And there isn't time for me to stand around here all day, pondering the meaning of true love and my deepest desires with some florist," she said while waving her hand in front of his body. "You have my email. Please send me a contract to review as soon as possible, and I will look over the details and send you a deposit."

He nodded and stood, again extending his hand to her.

Instead of taking it, she simply tugged her coat around her body, picked up the binder from the table, and twirled before leaving the workroom-and a stunned Lucas-behind.

Chapter One

Staring absently at a sticky note in front of her, Mya couldn't help but wonder exactly where her life went wrong. She should be preparing to walk down the aisle at St. Patrick's Cathedral in less than a week. Instead, she was frantically canceling vendors and working on notifying over 700 guests that the wedding had been canceled.

Pondering her past, she knew she loved Dave at some point in their relationship, and she thought he loved her, too. They were to have a marriage mostly of convenience, one that was laid out for them because of each of their families' statuses, but she did care for him. Since childhood, they had run in the same social circles of the New York City elite. They grew up going to the same prep schools and attending the same fundraising galas. He was her first kiss, and for much of their late teens and early twenties, they were inseparable.

Mya had known that their marriage wouldn't be spectacular, but she knew it would be tolerable, and she was okay with that. Complacent even. She was never the type of woman who believed in a happily ever after, but was the type of woman who knew she was expected to marry to keep her outstanding social status among the upper crust of New York City.

And while she didn't expect her life with Dave to be perfect, she did expect that they would each be faithful to one another, no matter how unspectacular their sex life was.

Yesterday, she stood in a dressing room for the last fitting on her $22,500 custom Pnina Tornai gown. The long-sleeve gown featured a stunning lace floral applique design, a plunging neckline, and an A-line skirt. For the first time in years, she actually felt beautiful when she looked in the mirror and saw her reflection staring back at her. She didn't feel like an imposter but instead felt like she truly belonged in the dress, belonged among the rich socialites and business moguls she so often rubbed elbows with.

That feeling had been short-lived when her phone rang, echoing through the fitting room. Digging her phone from her oversized Louis Vuitton shoulder bag, she was surprised to see a FaceTime request from Dave. Not one to normally call unless absolutely warranted, she immediately worried something was wrong and swiped across the screen to answer. Quickly, she could see something was wrong, just not in the sense she had expected. To her horror, staring back at her was a very naked Dave sitting on his large mahogany desk, an equally naked Charlene-her best friend and maid of honor-on top of him. It looked like one of the two had accidentally called her from his desktop computer at work while they were busy doing what could only be described as getting better acquainted with one another.

She quietly hung up, not letting on that she had seen what was happening before her eyes and removed herself from the designer gown before hastily leaving the designer bridal boutique. Calling out of work for the rest of the day, she arrived at her and Dave's penthouse less than twenty minutes later, a locksmith shortly behind. She hurriedly packed two suitcases full of Dave's belongings and left them with their doorman along with the five-carat cushion-cut engagement ring he had proposed to her with less than a year ago. And then, she began the daunting task of canceling a highly anticipated New York City wedding that was set to take place in six days.

The next day while sitting at her desk, Mya brought her attention back to the note in front of her, a daunting list of everything and everybody who needed to be notified the wedding had been canceled. As she drew a line through the word caterer, her phone pinged, signaling an incoming text.

Dave: **Mya, stop all of this and let's just talk! It wasn't what it looked like!**

She sighed before typing out a response, her resolve holding high.

Mya: **Really, Dave? It looked like you were playing a rousing game of hide the hotdog. Too little, too late. Please do not contact me again. Any money I am able to get back from the remaining vendors will be directly debited into the accounts which were originally used.**

Dave: **What will our parents think?**

A shrill laugh escaped her lips, and she was suddenly overcome with rage. The room around her turned to red as she picked up the phone, scrolled through her contacts, and tapped on Dave's name.

"Mya…"

She cut him off before he had the chance to continue.

"Don't Mya me, Dave. Listen to me, and listen close because I will not repeat myself. I've spent the majority of my life with you. I've sacrificed for you; I've changed for you-all so you could pursue your dreams while I put my own on the back burner. I knew we would never be perfect with our boring once-weekly missionary sex and our once-a-month date where we pretended like we loved each other for the good of being seen together, but looking back, I don't think either of us has loved each other for a long time. I just *never* expected you to stoop so low as to be unfaithful to me. And then, when you were unfaithful, it was with my best friend! Was that even the first time? How many others have there been on your business trips and late-night meetings?"

Mya continued, her voice growing louder and her words becoming more hurried. "I deserve to be loved, Dave. I deserve to be happy and challenged, not placated with gifts and false promises to keep me complacent. And don't use our parents to keep me trapped with you any longer. I won't do it anymore, and using their status and wealth isn't going to work any longer. I truly hope you find happiness, but it won't be with me."

· She ended the call without saying goodbye and returned once more to her to-do list. Sighing, a small bubble of dread crept up in her stomach as she saw the next vendor on her list-Winston's Flowers.

Mya had spoken with Lucas Gentry several times over the last few months of whirlwind wedding planning, and almost every interaction she had with the pompous florist left her furious. The man was basically born to push every one of her buttons every single time they communicated, and she was sure today would be no different.

"Just like ripping off a Band-Aid," she spoke softly, even though there wasn't anyone else in her office to hear her.

Picking up her purse, she exited her office, stopping by the reception desk on her way to the elevator. Charlotte, her personal assistant, wasn't at the desk, and upon scanning the area, Mya found the young woman watering plants in an office.

"How are you holding up?" she asked Mya.

Mya didn't have a lot of friends, but over the years that she had been working at Interior Aesthetic, she had grown close to Charlotte and often confided in her. This morning, Charlotte had taken one look at Mya with her kind eyes, and Mya immediately broke down into sobs for the first time since she decided she would not let Dave back into the home that had become theirs.

Mya let out a small but strained laugh. "I've been better, Char."

Charlotte gave her a weak smile, walking around the office to make sure no plant had been left unwatered. Mya continued. "I talked the caterer into still making all the food they were going to provide for our guests. I'm going to have it all donated to a few home-less shelters in the city."

"Oh, wow," Charlotte exclaimed as she looked at her friend with wide eyes, "That's really great Mya. I love how you always find a way to make even the worst disaster into something good."

"Honestly, I think the worst disaster would have been if I ended up actually marrying him. Is it horrible that I am almost thankful it happened?"

Charlotte cringed. "I'm just thankful you found out when you did. But still, I'm sorry it happened, and I'm here for whatever you need."

"I'm good for now; I really am. Can you just take any calls I get for a few hours? I need to go talk with the florist, and I feel like that is a conversation best had in person."

Charlotte's eyes widened. "Ohhh, the sexy Lucas Gentry? Maybe you should hop on that while you're there! Get yourself a sip from that tall glass of water!"

Mya scoffed, regretting that she had ever mentioned that the broad-shouldered florist may have been marginally good-looking. "That is the absolute *last* thing I would do."

Charlotte's giggle was almost contagious when she responded, "Never say never, Mya. Never say never!"

"Never!" It was all Mya said as she exited the office and walked toward the open elevator doors.

Twenty minutes later, Mya fought through the crowded subway car and ascended the steps of the 77th Street subway station into a torrential downpour. Cursing under her breath-she almost never cursed out loud-she felt the sudden rainstorm matched her mood. Without an umbrella, her usual hurried step was quickened even further, although it was no match for the rain. By the time she arrived under the awning of Winston's Flowers, her normal sleek bob was plastered to the sides of her face. The short sleeve silk blouse she wore was clinging to her body like a second skin, and she could wring the rain from her pencil skirt.

She pulled a silver compact from her handbag and flipped it open, not surprised to see her apparent waterproof mascara was nothing compared to the deluge she had just navigated. Wiping her fingers under her eyes, she was able to erase most of her raccoon eyes before rifling her fingers through her hair in an attempt to resurrect the flattened, wet mess.

Taking one last look at herself in the compact mirror, she hastily snapped it shut and haphazardly tossed it back into her purse.

That wasn't her, though. She didn't toss things haphazardly around. Everything had its place. She loved order. Just knowing that the compact wasn't in the exact place it was supposed to be inside her purse irked her. Mya counted to ten, trying desperately to ignore the nagging feeling inside her gut. But that feeling won out, and before she could stop herself, she reached back into her purse, took the compact out once again, and returned it to its rightful pocket inside the handbag.

Feeling only marginally better, she smoothed her skirt as best she could before reaching for the handle, the familiar bell above the door signaling her entrance into the flower shop.

Chapter Two

Lucas was helping an older gentleman create a custom bouquet for his wife's birthday when the rain had begun. The sound of raindrops and thunder had been so loud that it was almost impossible to hear the soft background music that played over the shop's speakers.

Summer thunderstorms on humid afternoons weren't unheard of in New York City, but this one brought along something unexpected. This one brought along Mya Monroe.

Mya was everything Lucas wasn't. She came from an affluent background of the New York City elite. Her clothes and accessories were always designer; the makeup on her skin was always impeccable-right down to the dark red Estee Lauder lipstick she wore religiously-and she never had a hair out of place. Lucas was fairly certain she was the type of woman who had her entire life planned for her since the day she was born and knew he was the very antithesis of her prim and proper planned life.

That didn't stop him from thinking about her, though. He thought of her almost as often as he inhaled breath and had since she first waltzed into his flower shop in an icy tizzy the previous November.

Lucas had thoughts about Mya that no man should have about a woman soon to marry another man. He had imagined what it would be like for Mya to straddle him, what it would feel like to slide into her pussy as she rode him, her small, handful-sized breasts rising and falling in time with their movements. He pictured those red lips wrapped around his cock as she obeyed his every command and dammit if he wasn't having those thoughts right now and becoming hard while trying to help the old man pick between roses and peonies.

While his mind had often been straying to the woman since she first entered his shop all those months ago, it wasn't the first time he had seen Mya. He actually first laid eyes on her almost two years prior at a wedding he worked. After delivering bouquets to the bridal party, he took a seat in the back of the large church, waiting for the ceremony to finish. Lucas liked to repurpose floral arrangements as often as possible and would regularly transport arrangements from a church to a reception location, hiding out in the back pew until he could make his move. It helped to create less waste, was more cost effective-not that most of his clientele cared about cost-and allowed him to make sure nothing was out of place right before the bride made her grand entrance.

As he sat in the last pew, his eyes were laser-focused on the most beautiful woman he had ever seen as she stood towards the front of the church talking with a few other guests. She wore a curve hugging silver dress that was covered in sequins, her inky black hair-longer at the time-was up in an elegant twist of some sort with small tendrils framing her heart shaped face. Her deep, red lips stood out against her creamy, pale skin. An underwhelmingly normal man stood at her side, his hand on her lower back, as he seemed to repeatedly break into her conversation, cutting her off mid-sentence. She almost looked defeated, and Lucas couldn't help but feel like this woman deserved to be with someone as magnificent as she was. Not that he thought himself magnificent, but this woman was straight fire and should be treated like a trophy, not as a simple bystander.

His eyes stayed on the back of her head throughout

the ceremony. He studied the long, elegant curve of her neck, studied how her shoulders curved down into perfectly toned arms. He cataloged every feature he could see throughout the ceremony and must have completely zoned out because suddenly, everyone around him was on their feet as the bridal party made their exit from the church. All eyes were on the party- all eyes but Mya who was staring directly back at Lucas with a questioning look on her face.

As soon as he realized she had caught him staring, he quickly averted his gaze, carefully adjusting the growing bulge in his pants before quietly exiting the pew to begin deconstructing flowers that hung from the pews and altar.

He didn't see her at the reception, although he scanned the room multiple times for her before he left. In fact, he didn't see her again until she came into his flower shop looking to plan her own wedding. Lucas would never blatantly make a pass at a married woman, even one as stunning as Mya. He just wasn't that kind of man. But damn, if he wasn't tempted.

He could see the small glimpse of sadness in her eyes when he had inquired into what it was she wanted when she came in for their initial consultation. He felt remorseful for her-sad that someone had taken so much joy from the woman that she wasn't even excited for what should be the happiest day of her life.

He never brought it up, never pressed the issue the few times they had spoken since that consultation. He preferred to keep conversation professional, even if he did want to know *so* much more about the raven-haired beauty, even if he wanted nothing more than to bury himself inside her and stay there for a solid week, only coming up for air when extremely necessary.

Lucas distractedly finished with the elderly man, all while keeping a watchful eye on Mya as she stood outside the large window to the flower shop. The rain continued to pound down from the heavens, but she made no effort to move from under the small awning that jutted from the building's brick exterior.

Finally, as he was ringing up the man's purchase, the bell above the door chimed, and Mya barged into the shop, water dripping from her hair and the soaked clothes that hung from her body. Only when the customer walked towards the door to exit the shop did she move from the doorway.

"Mr. Gentry."

Even when soaked from head to toe, disheveled from the rain, she was still beautiful, still poised with perfect posture and long, toned legs.

"Coming down like cats and dogs out there, eh?" He cringed at his own words and rolled his eyes with how cliché he sounded. Internally, he chided himself. He was a man who, on appearances alone, brought women to their knees without words, and here he was commenting on the weather like a fucking kid in elementary school.

She didn't answer the rhetorical question, instead took a few tentative steps in his direction leaving a trail of water behind her. "Do you have a few moments to speak, Mr. Gentry?"

An electric smile spread across his lips causing Mya to quickly notice his slightly imperfect front teeth, one of which appeared slightly chipped. "For you, I have as much time as you need. And it's Lucas."

She nodded curtly but made no effort to come closer until he spoke again. "Come on; we can talk in the back."

Mya finally found her footing and followed Lucas to the workroom she had been in before. He asked April, the girl who welcomed Mya on her first visit to Winston's Flowers, to cover the floor and then walked to the rear of the room, opening a few cabinets before finding what he was looking for. He came to stand in front of Mya, a towel in his outstretched arm. She graciously accepted and began patting her hair and clothing dry while Lucas perched on a nearby stool.

Their eyes locked, an electric current passing through them that Mya had never noticed before. The feeling took her by surprise, and she quickly glanced away, replacing the small smile that had crept across her face by pressing her lips together into a tight line.

"You're just a few days away from your big day now. Are you coming in to check up on me? Afraid I'm not doing my job right?"

Mya's face dropped, her usual steely resolve slipping as she stared at a point somewhere over his right shoulder. It was only then that Lucas took inventory of Mya, searching for what had the usual lioness of a woman distracted. She placed the towel on the table and twisted her hands together in front of her, causing his eyes to fall on her long, slim fingers. One finger, in particular, caught his eye as he noticed the engagement ring the size of a small iceberg that normally adorned her left ring finger was missing.

Without thinking, he reached out, taking her hands in his. Surprisingly, she didn't pull away. It wasn't until that very moment that she realized just how desperate she was for simple human touch.

His need to be in control took over. "Talk to me. Tell me what's going on." It wasn't a question, but a quiet command.

Mya pulled her hands out of his grasp, taking in a deep, cleansing breath. "Simply put, there isn't going to be a wedding. I understand that it is far too late for any type of refund, and I am absolutely okay with that. But what can be done? Can you use the flowers that were going to be used in my arrangements? Can you sell them to other people? I have no idea how any of this works."

Lucas pushed himself off the stool. "Give me just a sec to grab your file, and we'll see what we can figure out. Can you hang out for a few while we go over everything together?"

He didn't wait for her to answer.

Mya couldn't help but notice how calm he was as he walked into a small office situated off the work-room. Surely, he didn't get an influx of jilted brides-to-be looking to cancel almost $75,000 worth of flowers six days before their weddings.

He returned less than a minute later, file in hand. Reclaiming his place on the stool, he opened the file and thumbed through a few pages as Mya looked on. "Almost everything needed for the wedding has already been ordered or delivered to the shop and is waiting in the walk-in coolers to be assembled. Some of the stock can be used in traditional arrangements that are sold here, so it won't be a total wash. The rest, well…to be honest, the rest will probably end up getting trashed."

Mya cringed outwardly. She wasn't upset about the money that was wasted but was appalled to know that these flowers would simply end up in a dumpster. She searched her brain for a better solution while her eyes searched Lucas's eyes in a silent plea to not let the flowers go to waste.

Long, silent seconds passed between the two before Mya spoke. "I hate that. Do you have any other weddings planned that you could incorporate some of the flowers into? Maybe a bride who couldn't have her dream wedding but could if some of these flowers were used?"

Lucas thought, tapping a pen cap against his lips as he did. "Let me make a few phone calls tonight and see what I can come up with. Generally speaking, if someone is coming to Winston's for their wedding, they're not worried about the cost associated with their wedding. But that doesn't mean we can't figure something out."

Mya held out her hand to Lucas and only spoke when he hesitated to take it. "Thank you, Mr. Gentr., I just cannot fathom everything ending up in the garbage because my now ex-fiancé was stupid enough to get caught cheating six days before our wedding with my best friend."

She clasped a hand over her mouth the second the words crossed her lips, embarrassment flushing over her cheeks.

Lucas tried to play it cool, tried to act like that small vulnerability she accidentally showed didn't affect him, like he didn't want to hunt down this now ex-fiancé of hers and rearrange his features into a Picasso painting for hurting this stunning woman standing in front of him. "I'll call you tomorrow once I have a game plan in place-if that is okay with you?"

Mya was afraid to speak again, afraid more words would come tumbling from her normally tight-lipped mouth. Instead of words, she gave Lucas a curt nod before striding out of the workroom and back into the rainy New York City afternoon.

Lucas stared in her direction for several minutes after she left, his mind repeatedly going back over what she unexpectedly told him. From their few interactions, he knew she wasn't the type of person who opened up easily. In fact, the woman was a total ice queen. She seemed to be a pro at keeping people at arms' length, and Lucas wondered if it had something to do with her long-term relationship with her now ex. He was surprised she acted upset knowing that her unused wedding flowers would mostly end up in the trash. It contradicted her normally cool demeanor. But now, knowing how much the thought upset Mya, he was determined to find the perfect way to use her flowers to bring as much happiness to other people. Just maybe, he could melt the ice queen in the process, too.

Chapter Three

Mya had spent the afternoon on-site, finishing a project for a trendy boutique hotel that would soon open in Bowery. The neighborhood had a rough past full of homelessness, prostitution, and gangs that dated back to the mid-1800s and even housed the famous CBGB club where infamous punk rock bands like The Ramones and Talking Heads often played. However, since the 1990s, the area saw an influx of new money that brought along high-rise condominiums, luxury developments, hotels, and a younger, more hip crowd that reveled in the neighborhood's gritty history. The Bowery Alliance of Neighbors, a grassroots organization local to the neighborhood, had played a huge role in the transformation of the area by providing property developers incentive to restore old buildings as opposed to demolishing them which helped to keep the historic feel of the area.

Mya loved seeing the revitalization happening and felt honored to play a small part in the overall large-scale project. It had taken almost two years for the construction to be complete on the old twenty-four-story brick building before her company was hired to complete the interior design work needed. She was heading up the common areas throughout the space including a rooftop bar, two restaurants, a reception and concierge area, and a small sitting area on each floor. She had worked tirelessly with the hotel owner, and together, they decided the hotel would pay homage to the neighborhood's history with oversized black and white canvas photographs depicting the neighborhood throughout the years. She picked these photos to give hotel guests a small look into the past, choosing to only source images from past and present photographers who called Bowery home.

She was standing on the outside terrace that was nestled on the top floor of the hotel. Surveying her surroundings, she took in the classic old-world style the area conjured with intricately tiled floors, ivy-covered brick exterior walls, and an oversized glazed fireplace. Mya added sleek metal lamps and soft throw pillows on the outdoor furniture to balance the history of the building with the fresh new feel the hotel developer was looking to create within the space. She was up to her proverbial eyeballs rearranging furniture to shape the perfect cozy yet inviting space when her phone trilled, signaling an incoming call.

Pushing a few stray hairs out of her eye, she walked to a large built-in bar that jutted from the side of the brick, picking up her phone from it just before it stopped ringing.

So caught up in her day, she had forgotten that Lucas Gentry was to call her today and was only reminded when his gruff voice spoke from the other end of her cell.

"I was able to come up with a few things I think could work for your flowers."

Mya sighed, relief washing over her body. "Mr. Gentry, I can't thank you enough. I'm sure whatever you have determined will be much better than the alternative."

He let out a rumble of a laugh in response that took Mya by surprise. "One of these days, Ms. Monroe, you'll actually call me Lucas." He paused waiting for a response, but when none came, he continued to speak. "And actually, I haven't completely finalized the plans yet; I could use your help with that. What are the chances I could convince you to have dinner with me tonight so I can show you what I have in mind?"

Lucas was thankful at that moment that he was on the other side of the phone and not face-to-face with Mya. Did he really just ask her to have dinner with him under the guise of finalizing plans for her failed wedding flowers? He cringed inwardly but made no haste to rebuke on the invite of dinner. He had to see her again, and he wasn't completely lying when he said he needed her help with finalizing the plans for what would happen with her overly expensive yet not needed flowers.

She huffed, and he couldn't say that her response was unexpected. Mya Monroe was a hard shell, but damn if he didn't want to see beneath that steely exterior. He wanted to know just what made her tick, what made passion pour from her soul, what turned her on.

He stopped himself from thinking any further as that last thought crossed his mind.

"Against my better judgment," her voice held her familiar no-nonsense tone, "I will agree to dinner with you because I want nothing more than to put this all behind me."

Mya glanced at her reflection in a nearby window and then returned her attention to the phone. "Does 7:00 P.M. work for you? I have a few things to finish in

Bowery before stopping by my office. Then I will need to stop by my apartment..."

Lucas could have been imagining things, but suddenly, he thought he heard just an ounce of nervousness in her voice. Before she could continue or worse yet, change her mind, he cut her off. "Seven sounds great. How about you shoot me a text and let me know where to meet you. This is my cell. I'll be coming right from the shop, so just give me enough time to get to where you need me."

Where you need me? Did he actually just say that? God, he couldn't speak to this woman without unintentionally hitting on her. And she had been single for all of forty-eight hours.

They said their goodbyes while he quietly chastised himself, promising to keep himself reigned in during their dinner. He knew that was a lie, knew he was already going to press her buttons harder than he ever had before.

Mya placed her phone back on the bar and returned to work although she felt distracted for the rest of her day.

When she entered the office building later that afternoon, Charlotte greeted her from her desk in the reception area the moment the elevator doors opened. Always eager and optimistic, Charlotte was an amazing personal assistant to have and an even better friend.

"Hey Mya," she cheerfully chirped. "How's the Bowery Boutique going?"

Mya leaned against the desk, filling Charlotte in on the progress she made throughout the day. She was halfway to her office before she turned back to Charlotte. "Hey, could you make me a reservation for seven tonight at Stefano's? Two people."

"Please tell me you are *not* having dinner with Dave," the girl all but whined.

Mya laughed. "Oh, absolutely not."

"And…are you going to tell me who you *are* having dinner with? You know I hate knowing that you have other friends that aren't me."

She rolled her eyes at her friend. "No, because you will make it into something it isn't."

Charlotte's eyes widened, almost making her appear bug-eyed. "Oh, come on, Mya! Now I *really* want to know!"

"Lucas Gentry," Mya said, pausing for a moment to allow Charlotte time to have the monumental freak-out Mya knew she would have. "He has been kind enough to help me finalize plans for repurposing the flowers from the wedding. He simply needed additional input from me and asked if we could meet to complete that task tonight."

Charlotte laughed. "Oh, and it just so happens that he needed to ask you out to dinner to take care of that task?" She threw the word "task" in air quotes.

Until that minute, Mya hadn't thought anything of it. She just assumed that Mr. Gentry-Lucas-was as anxious as she was to put the entire fiasco behind them. She wasn't exactly looking forward to dinner with the flower shop owner, but surprisingly enough, she wasn't absolutely dreading it either. In fact, knowing that the last thing she needed to handle from her now-defunct wedding was soon to be complete made her feel like maybe she could start to move on.

Suddenly, though, Mya's stomach flip-flopped, and her palms grew clammy. She wasn't sure if it was knowing that after tonight, the last remnants of her relationship with Dave would be gone, but something was just…off.

Looking back to Charlotte who was still staring at her in disbelief, she took a deep, cleansing breath before speaking. "Seven, two people, Stefano's Restaurant." She turned around and quickly finished the short walk to her office, a dramatic sigh cascading from her lips as she fell backwards into the wingback chair that sat in the corner of her office.

Not one thing got accomplished the rest of the day as Mya stared idly at her computer screen. Usually, she was a workhorse, a force to be reckoned with when it came to deadlines and projects. Most days, she beat Charlotte to the office in the morning, and it was rare that she left for the day before the sun had long but set. Today, though, she logged out of her computer, grabbed her purse, and waltzed past the reception area without saying goodnight to her friend at exactly 5:00 P.M.

Mya hurriedly strolled the few blocks to the subway station, swimming through the other commuters carving their way through the hundreds of midtown tourists. While she had been born in New York City, the atmosphere never ceased to send lightning through her veins. She loved the sounds of taxi horns honking at all hours, the steam wafting up from subway grates in the winter, and the transformation of color that spread across the vast city each spring. Many days throughout the summer, she even found herself walking the twenty-something city blocks to her Upper East Side penthouse. Today, though, she chose to take the subway, eager to get home and shower the day off before meeting with Lucas.

Walking the last few blocks to her apartment, she gave a small wave to the elderly doorman before she climbed into a private elevator car, swiped her access card, and pushed the button indicating the penthouse floor.

Her apartment was an extension of her, until

recently, perfectly proper life. Every carefully selected knick-knack and tchotchke were perched in the perfect place to showcase their beauty, not a stray speck of dust on any surface. She liked her penthouse well enough, but for the first time, looking around the open space made her feel hollow inside instead of welcomed. It was beautiful with its floor-to-ceiling windows and sweeping views of Central Park. The living room led to a wrap-around terrace that Mya had covered with precisely enough greenery to give it an earthy feel and the kitchen could be the envy of any professional chef- not that Mya knew how to cook anything more than the most basic spaghetti.

When she first moved into the space, she had dreamt of entertaining in the open concept living and dining area. She longed to sit at the Steinway & Sons grand piano, playing music for her family around the holidays. She had plans of huge, elegant meals with family and friends where laughter filled the house.

None of those dreams ever happened though, and while she loved the carefully curated apartment, she couldn't help but feel that the penthouse was simply too big for one person. She could continue to pay for the space with her own salary while dipping into a trust fund set up by her parents; she just didn't know if she wanted to.

The concept hit her like a ton of bricks as she

defeatedly trudged to the massive ensuite bathroom. As if on autopilot, she undressed and stepped under the multi-head shower, warm water pelting her skin as it cascaded around her. The white-tiled bathroom was her sanctuary, and she wanted nothing more than to fill up the oversized tub with almost-scalding water and soak in a eucalyptus-scented bath while wallowing in self-pity. And she almost did. It would have been easy to text Lucas and cancel their dinner meeting, to tell him to just throw away the flowers he couldn't use, but something deep within her body told her this was important and something she couldn't brush off.

Mya begrudgingly pulled herself from the stream of water and lightly toweled off before dressing in a black pencil skirt and loose, sleeveless, deep purple blouse. Quickly she dried her hair and applied minimal makeup, adding her favorite Estee Lauder lipstick in the shade Rouge Excess before sliding her feet into a matching purple pair of pointed-toe Manolo Blahnik pumps.

She took one last look around her penthouse before picking up her purse from the small table in the entry-way. And then, she made the short walk to Stefano's where she would begin to put the past behind her.

Chapter Four

ACCORDING to Mya's silver Movado watch, it was 6:54 P.M. when she arrived at Stefano's. She detested being late almost as much as she detested those gaudy smart watches most everyone else her age swore by.

Opening the door to the restaurant, she was pleasantly surprised to find Lucas already waiting in the small vestibule that led to the hostess station. Mya was used to seeing Lucas in his flower shop attire of jeans and a flannel button-up, an apron tied around his neck and back. Tonight, though, Lucas the flower shop owner was gone, and in his place stood a man in fitted black slacks, a charcoal gray dress shirt with the sleeves rolled up, and a deep aubergine bow tie. Although he said he was coming straight from work, it appeared he made time to change before their meeting.

She closed the space between them, extending her hand. As he slid his hand over hers, he gestured between them with his opposite hand. "Look at us already wearing matching outfits."

Mya's face contorted in confusion for half a second before it fell back to its usual neutral state, realization setting in that he was referring to both of them wearing some shade of purple.

In true Mya fashion, her response was clipped and slightly cold. "There are a finite number of colors in the world. Surely it was bound to happen at some point, Mr. Gentry."

Lucas was unaffected by her unwillingness to let her guard down. He always prided himself on not backing down from a challenge. And damn, was Mya Monroe a challenge.

After checking in with the hostess, they were led to their intimate two-top table near the back of the restaurant. Mya followed behind the hostess, Lucas behind her. He tried to tell himself that he was doing the gentlemanly thing by allowing her to lead, but in reality, he was using the short walk to the table as an excuse to check out her gorgeous round ass in her tight pencil skirt. The woman didn't just walk; she floated with a gentle sway of her hips. Long legs led to stiletto-clad feet, and in her tall heels, she stood almost at eye level with him.

They approached the table, and Lucas pulled out one of the chairs, motioning at Mya to sit before taking the seat across from her. The restaurant was busy, but the low chatter of customers around them did nothing to take away from the gentle ambiance of their surroundings. Low lighting filled the space while candles flickered on each table. Mellow music piped through speakers, the Rat Pack filling the air around them. The scent of freshly baked bread wafted through the dining room, making Mya feel both warm and hungry at the same time.

Their waiter appeared, and after a small amount of convincing, Mya uncharacteristically allowed Lucas to order her beverage for her. It gave him a small satisfaction that she relinquished even the most minuscule amount of control. God only knew he wanted to control all of her.

When the waiter retreated from the table, Mya turned her gaze to Lucas.

"Okay, Mr. Gentry, can we discuss exactly what your plans are?"

A salacious grin spread across Lucas's face as he studied Mya for a minute longer than necessary. His hand came up to rub across his rough beard. "Oh, Ms. Monroe," he said in a low cadence, leaning in closer to her, "I don't think you could handle knowing what my exact plans are."

Mya became obviously flustered as a slow blush crept up her cheeks. Fuck, if it wasn't fun for Lucas to get under this woman's skin.

And he wanted to get under her skin. Or, at least under her clothes. He backed off though, knowing what he was about to present to her would very likely have her running for the hills before their main course was even served. He didn't want to scare her off prematurely.

The server returned with their wine-a 2017 Kathryn Hall Cabernet Sauvignon from Napa. After swirling the dark red liquid in her glass, Mya sipped the wine, allowing it to play over her tongue before swallowing. She was impressed with the choice as an earthy and spicy blend of flavors smoothly cascaded down her throat. She arched a brow in Lucas's direction, and he was convinced he saw the slightest uptick on the corner of her lips.

Lucas held his glass to hers, and after slight hesitation on Mya's end, they lightly clinked their glasses to one another. "You look surprised," he said while a grin splayed across his face.

Taking another sip of her wine, Mya nodded. "I admit, I am a bit surprised. Where did you learn about wine, Mr. Gentry?"

"It's Lucas," he corrected her before continuing. "Before I took over the family business, I worked at an upscale wine bar. I learned a lot in the few years I worked there. Did you know there are five basic characteristics of wine?"

Mya unconsciously tossed her head back and forth, as if trying to recall something from the depths of her brain. Listing off each characteristic on her fingers, she spoke them aloud, "Body, alcohol, sweetness…" She trailed off and looked to Lucas when she couldn't recall the last two.

"Acidity and tannin," he supplied. "I'm impressed. Three out of five isn't too shabby."

"Three out of five wouldn't be a passing grade," Mya dryly retorted.

His eyes slipped from her gaze, dropping down to her slightly parted red lips before returning to her hazel eyes. "Good thing we're not in class then, Mya." He gave her a wink, and she shifted uncomfortably in her seat in response.

Their waiter brought out their appetizers, and Lucas watched as Mya daintily cut into a stack of fresh basil, mozzarella, and tomato before sliding the fork into her mouth. He couldn't help but find himself transfixed as her lips wrapped around the tines of the fork, and for a slight second, he wished he were that very piece of silverware.

She broke his thoughts when she spoke, gesturing with her fork to a manilla folder that sat off to the side of the table. "Can we please cut to the chase?"

He slowly slid the folder in front of him, his finger trailing along the side of it teasingly, before opening the file. "So, you're saying you're *not* having a good time just chatting with me, *Mya*?"

An uncomfortable silence fell between the two, the file teasingly sitting open, taunting Mya.

She couldn't recall a time he had used her first name when speaking with her before. Sure, it had probably happened, but she was almost always Ms. Monroe to him. And he certainly hadn't used such a playful tone before. That she was sure of. It left her feeling slightly uneasy as she simply continued to stare at him, waiting for him to continue.

Lucas took a large bite of his white bean and prosciutto bruschetta. "Want one?" he asked, pushing the plate towards her.

Her only response was an exasperated sigh.

He chuckled and then finally pulled a few pieces of paper from the file and slid them towards Mya. She started looking over them as he spoke, but the contacts and language throughout might as well have been written in hieroglyphics. They made absolutely no sense to Mya, and she could feel her frustration building even further. "I won't lie; I had ordered a metric shit-ton of flowers for you, and I don't know that I will be able to repurpose all of them." Her shoulders slightly slumped, but Lucas kept speaking. "I have a proposition for you, and I want you to hear me out with an open mind."

She cocked an eyebrow at him as the waiter approached their table once again. Dropping off their main courses-tortellini carbonara for Mya and veal ossobuco for Lucas. It was only after he left the side of their table that they resumed their mainly one-sided conversation.

"I donate quite a bit of time and resources to charity events that are special to me each year." He took a bite of his meal, savoring the taste, quickly swallowing it before continuing. Mya sat, a singular tortellini speared through her fork, unable to bring it to her mouth.

Lucas tapped one of the papers in front of her. "Next month, I am helping with the Night of a Million Stars gala. Have you heard of it?"

Mya nodded. As someone of her social standing, she had attended the gala for several years with her family, and more recently with Dave. It was one of the largest events of the year, and everything raised went to children in foster care throughout New York City. Two years ago, she won a weeklong trip to Aspen during the silent auction, and last year, a privately chartered yacht for a week in the Caribbean.

"This is the first year I have been asked to give my time to the organization. It is important to me that I do well, and that is where you come in."

Mya still hadn't taken a bite of her meal, though Lucas casually ate his like they weren't having this extremely odd conversation. She stared at him, unable to predict where he was going with his request.

He pulled another piece of paper from the folder, sliding it towards Mya. Their fingers brushed as she took it from him, and the small hairs on the back of her neck stood on end in response. She took a minute to read through the paper in front of her, and as she did, her eyes continued to widen.

Slowly pushing the paper away from her, she raised her gaze to find Lucas already staring at her patiently. "You…you are out of your mind." The words came out hushed.

"Am I?"

She laughed, slightly manically. "Let me get this straight, Mr. Gentry. You want me to help you with the event, and in return, you will forfeit the balance of my original event cost and return that to me?"

"That is part of the arrangement, yes."

"And what is the rest of the arrangement?"

He looked at the paper that now sat between them

as he popped another bite of his main course into his mouth. Scanning the document upside down, he found what he was looking for and tapped it, bringing Mya's attention to his finger. "Over the next month, you will help me with flower arrangements and delivery to several long-term care facilities throughout the city. Then, next month, you will attend the event with me. As my date. You will be mine, for one month."

Mya cackled now, causing a few heads to turn in their direction. "Absolutely not, Mr. Gentry."

He was undeterred and had the audacity to reach out and snag a tortellini from her plate, popping it into his mouth. "That's fucking delicious. You really should eat before it gets cold."

She pushed her chair back from the table, fully prepared to stand and walk away from the table, away from Lucas Gentry.

"Don't make a scene. Sit back down."

His voice was oddly commanding, and her body defied her mind when she pulled herself back towards the table.

"I'll tell you what, *Mya,*" he stretched her name out as if playing with the syllables as they rolled over his tongue. "Take this with you." He collected the papers from the table, placed them back into the folder, and slid it toward her. "Enjoy dinner with me tonight." He lightly slid her plate a few inches closer to her, grabbing another tortellini from her plate with a wink as he did. "Then when you get home tonight, you're going to pour yourself a glass of wine, maybe put on some low music, slide that beautiful body of yours into a nice hot bath. And then, you're going to read through everything here. Tomorrow, you're going to call me and tell me what you've decided."

Mya flushed, heat moving up her cheeks when she realized Lucas had called her body beautiful. The heat she was feeling wasn't from arousal though. It was pure anger. She was appalled that he thought he could use her for whatever his personal agenda was, horrified that he expected her to simply roll over and agree to be his date for one of the most extravagant galas of the year, one that her family and ex-fiané would most certainly be attending. Outraged that he expected to use her for labor and God only knew what else leading up to the gala. Like she didn't already have enough on her plate with her own job, Lucas wanted her to work for him, too.

The waiter chose that minute to come to their table, saving Mya from having to speak to Lucas. She took the opportunity to regain her composure, pushing her chair back as she stood from the table. Mya locked eyes with Lucas, silently daring him to try and stop her from leaving before she simply picked up her purse that had been hanging on the chairback. Sliding the bag over her shoulder, she started to walk away. She was almost away from the table when a hand roughly snaked around her wrist. Hackles raised, Mya turned back to Lucas, fire blazing in her eyes. He held her wrist a second longer, his fingers searing into her skin with electricity. Lucas dropped his hand, allowing her wrist to fall back to her side. Looking at him once more with an impassive gaze, she reached across the table, almost as if in slow motion, pulled the paperwork-filled folder to herself, and walked out of the restaurant like a woman with purpose.

Chapter Five

It was 8:03 P.M. when Mya arrived back at her penthouse. Tossing her purse onto the small table in the entryway, she didn't even care when it fell off and tumbled to the floor, spilling its contents. That was how angry Lucas Gentry had made her. Less than an hour and a half in his presence, she was ready to sell all her personal belongings, move to a remote island, and spend the rest of her days away from anyone who had ever heard of the name Lucas Gentry or Winston's Flowers.

Walking into the immaculate kitchen, Mya poured herself a healthy glass of wine before lowering the zipper on her skirt. She plodded back to the entryway, picking up her phone and file folder from the pile on the floor. Depositing herself on the luxe white leather sectional, she swiped open the messaging app on her phone and tapped out a message to Charlotte.

Mya: **Want to get drunk and eat ice cream with me**?

Mya watched three dots bounce on the bottom of the screen before Charlotte texted back, almost immediately,

Charlotte: **Oh damn, did dinner go that badly?**

Mya: **You have no fucking clue.**

Charlotte: **You just cursed. On purpose. I can be there in 20. I'll grab our boys on the way.**

Almost exactly twenty minutes later, the doorman rang the penthouse, announcing Charlotte's arrival. When the elevator door opened into the space, she found Mya still sitting on the couch, a glass of wine in hand, shirt untucked from her skirt, no shoes in sight. She walked towards her friend and held out a bag full of their boys-the boys being Ben and Jerry's Ice Cream in every assorted flavor possible.

Charlotte didn't waste time, pulling out each pint of ice cream, lining them up on the glass-top coffee table. She laughed when Mya pulled several coasters from a stylish basket on a nearby end table, placing one under each of the pints that had already been set atop the table. Even when she was stressed to the point of wanting to pull her hair from her scalp, Mya was worried about unsightly rings on her coffee table.

Mya dug into a pint of Cherry Garcia while Charlotte slid her spoon into some Phish Food. Looking to her friend, Charlotte stuck her spoon towards Mya, mouth full of half-melted ice cream. "Spill it, woman."

Mya recounted every painstaking detail from the night, starting with Lucas choosing their wine selection to how angry she was that she didn't get to eat one single tortellini from her meal. She told her friend about his proposition, how he kept sneaking food from her plate, and how he shamelessly flirted with her, going as far as to call her body beautiful.

Wide-eyed, Charlotte nodded along to the story, listening intently as Mya recounted the events. When she finished, Charlotte spoke without hesitation, "So, you're going to do it, right?"

Mya laughed, a full-on belly rumbling laugh that shook her entire body. She exchanged her pint of ice cream for her wine glass, taking a long sip of the crisp white wine. "Absolutely not."

Charlotte wasn't about to let her friend off easy. "Seriously, Mya? $75,000 is a lot of money, even to you. And all you have to do is meet up with him a few times and go with him to a gala that you would most likely already be going to."

Her friend wasn't wrong. $75,000 would allow her to stay in the penthouse-if that is what she decided to do-without having to touch her trust fund for a few extra months. It would allow her time to come up with a more foolproof plan than she currently had, which was absolutely nothing.

Mya retreated to her bedroom, finally changing from her skirt into simple black yoga pants and a faded Parsons School of Design tee, while Charlotte poured them each another oversized glass of wine. Both women settled back on the couch, Charlotte making herself comfortable by stretching out on one end of the sectional, legs draped over the arm of the couch.

Reluctantly, Mya picked up the file folder and began to finger the pages that were tucked inside. There were several pages of what she thought were contracts, that upon closer inspection turned out to be correspondence between Winston's Flowers and the Night of a Million Stars gala. Every painstaking detail was laid out in front of her, from the number of flowers that would be used to the types of arrangements requested to fit their theme. She was surprised to find multiple pages full of gorgeous floral sketches, possible renderings of what would be created for the night. She couldn't help but admire how beautiful the sketches were. Mya knew Lucas was talented, and if he had also drawn these sketches-well, she was impressed to say the least.

Charlotte made grabby hands at Mya from across the couch, indicating that she wanted to see what was given to her from the steamy florist. Mya obliged.

Her personal assistant turned friend spent several minutes looking through everything in the folder, making small comments on the flowers or gala before picking up one specific page. She eyed it for what seemed like an eternity before darting up in her seat, eyes wide and looking at Mya.

"Holy. Freaking. Shit." Charlotte's voice was shrill as she shrieked, the words bouncing off the walls of the living room as she held out a scrap of paper towards her friend. "How did you not tell me about this? Mya, you've been holding out on me, girl! You *have* to do this. It's fucking fate!"

Mya had no idea what the other woman was talking about. Reaching out to take the paper, she quickly scanned the words, not allowing them to fully sink in. It was only on her second read-through that she took the time to absorb the words that had been scribbled across the lined piece of notebook paper.

Mya,

It has been over two years since I first laid eyes on you, and while I never expected to see you again, I have thought of you almost daily since. The day you walked into my shop, you took my breath away all over again. I expected to do my job and let you go, but fate seemed to have had other plans.

I've seen the sadness in your eyes. The sadness you keep hidden behind that ice queen demeanor. I know there is a woman in there dying to be cared for and treated well.

Give me the chance by spending the next month with me, and I'll show you how a real man treats a woman, a woman like you.

Yours,

Lucas

Mya read the note a third time, then a fourth. Finally lowering it from her eyes, she looked at her friend in bewilderment. "When…" her words came out slightly shaky and breathy, "when did he see me before?"

Charlotte simply shrugged, "I don't know, babe, but you *have* to do it and find out."

Mya's mind was reeling. It very rarely was quiet, but at this moment, it was traveling at lightning speed. Questions swirled in her head. When had she met Lucas in the past? Had she spoken to him? What did he know about treating a woman like her? What did he even mean when he said that?

Charlotte downed the rest of her wine, placing the empty glass on the table without a coaster. She stood before speaking to her friend in a quiet tone. "I think you have a lot to think about, Mya. I really hope that you decide to do this. I think it could be good for you. I think *he* could be good for you."

Mya escorted her friend to the elevator, hugging her before she left for the night. Then, she stood in the penthouse, alone again. She surveyed her surroundings, empty ice cream cartons and wine bottles lining the table. And then, in an uncharacteristic move, she left everything on the table and went into her bedroom.

It was almost midnight, but for some reason, Lucas's words from dinner kept swirling through her mind. Stripping the clothes from her body, she filled the oversized bathtub with water that was almost too hot before she slid into the water. Lavender bubbles floated on the surface around her, clinging to her body. "Slide that beautiful body of yours into a nice hot bath," he had told her. And even though he wasn't there to make sure she obliged, she felt it necessary to do as he told.

She relaxed in the tub for several minutes, suddenly unaware of what her hands were doing. She unconsciously slid her hand off the side of the tub, bringing it down to the flesh between her legs. Mya ran a finger through her folds, searching for that little bundle of nerves. She hadn't touched herself in years, never felt the urge. But tonight, between the wine and the swirling thoughts of Lucas invading her mind, her hands couldn't help but wander her body.

She slid two slim fingers inside her depths, a small gasp passing her lips as she slowly pushed herself further towards the edge. Sliding back out, she ran small, slow circles over her clit before adding more pressure to her movements.

Mya's other hand roamed from her neck, down her collarbone, and over her breast. Ever so gently, she rolled her nipple between two fingers, feeling it harden beneath her touch. She squeezed at the little bud, lightly at first, then harder, almost to the point of pain.

She wanted to feel. What that feeling was, she wasn't sure. Pain? Pleasure? She didn't know, but damn, she knew she wanted to feel something. And this was something.

Eyes closed, sensation overtook her mind a short time later as an orgasm coursed through her body. Thrumming with the sensation of her hands on her tits and pussy, she cried out into the silence of the stark bathroom. Her breathing became ragged, spasms coursing through her body, and as she came, she felt something while her thoughts drifted to the florist who wanted to make her his.

Chapter Six

In almost seven years at Interior Aesthetic, Mya could count the number of days she had called out on one hand. Today had been one of those days. When her alarm blared at 5:45 A.M., she sat up, head swimming with a fierce wine hangover, and quickly sent her boss an email, letting the older woman know she would not be making it into the office.

Mya also couldn't remember the last time she had foregone her normal smoothie of bananas, berries, and leafy dark greens for something fried and greasy. Today, she was going to change that. In fact, today she was confident she was going to change quite a few things about her life.

One of the best parts of living in New York City was that everything was basically at her fingertips, even this early in the morning. A quick phone call to her building's concierge and she was rewarded a short time later with a delivery of pancakes, a broccoli cheese omelet, bacon, and freshly squeezed orange juice. She ate on the couch, not her normal chair at the kitchen island, and turned on the television while she stuffed herself full. *Nailed It*, Mya's guilty pleasure, played in the background. The show almost seemed out of place playing in such an ostentatious place, but Mya could relate to the poor bakers who tried-and most often failed-to create perfection in the kitchen. In fact, she felt that way about much of her life.

She had tried to sculpt a perfect life for herself, but in the end, where did it leave her? She didn't even have a gold sequined baker's hat to show for her efforts.

Sure, she had a job she liked well enough, even if interior design wasn't her first choice. Mya thought back on her childhood, on her dreams of wanting to be an artist-adream that was quickly squashed by her parents. They had constantly criticized her love of painting, going as far as to confiscate the brushes and buttery thick oil paints she received as a birthday gift from her grandparents for her fourteenth birthday when they thought she was spending too much time in front of canvases. It was a hobby, they told her, nothing she could ever make a career out of. So, she locked her love of the artform away and chose to focus on something that would make her parents slightly happier. They had still expected more from her, but in their eyes, at least she wasn't a starving artist. Mya hadn't picked up a brush in years. She missed the feel of one in her hands, the way the paint felt as it glided over a new canvas, the way she started with something blank and melded it into something full of beauty.

Her relationship with Dave had been much the same as her love of painting. It was something molded by both of their parents. They had each been groomed to New York City high society, and for a few years of her life, she thought it was a life she wanted. Dave seemed to fit the mold so effortlessly, a high-powered business man who traveled as often as he was at home. He was happy to schmooze at events, determined to continue to climb the corporate ladder.

Together, they had money and status, but sitting in her empty penthouse now, she knew neither was what she wanted from her life.

Mya cleaned the remnants of her wine and ice cream-infused night, taking special care to wipe the table of any lingering rings that had been left on the table. The whole time, she formulated a plan in her head on how to bring happiness back into her own life.

Not one to usually leave the house looking anything

but perfect, Mya felt slightly uncomfortable when she left the penthouse a few hours later wearing nothing but skinny jeans, a loose floral tank, and sandals. Of course, the sandals were Saint Laurent and the Bruno Cucinelli tank had cost more than some people spent each month on rent. However, she still felt under-dressed, and it showed in the way she pulled her arms around her body as she walked towards the small, independently-owned art store she passed almost daily on her way to the subway station.

She entered the tiny shop, instantly greeted by a young girl with blue hair and too many visible tattoos to count. Mya gave her a small nod, picking up a basket from the entrance before navigating to an aisle filled with rows and rows of paints. Fingering tubes of various brands and colors, she loaded up on Williamsburg Handmade oil paints, filling her basket with almost every color imaginable until they spilled over the edge. Taking the basket to the register, she told the young woman she would be back before picking up another basket.

Soon, she approached the register again, this basket filled with brushes, a few paint palettes, several small palette and painting knives, primer, and brush cleaning accessories. The sales clerk looked at her as if she had multiple heads when she set the second overflowing basket atop the counter, telling her once again that she would return in just a few minutes.

At last, Mya returned to the counter for a third time, her arms full of stretched canvases of different sizes. She pointed to an easel along the wall, indicating to the girl she also wanted to add it to her growing pile of art supplies. The sales girl briskly worked through the baskets, her eyes continuing to widen as the total on her screen climbed. Scanning the canvases and inputting the easel, she let out a small gasp before reading the total to Mya who handed over a Black American Express card without hesitation.

Thankfully for Mya, most of what she picked was small enough to fit in several large bags, and though cumbersome, she was able to hoist the box the easel came in under one arm while handling the rest of her purchases in the other. Profusely thanking the sales girl, she not so gracefully pushed her way out into the street and started to walk towards her next stop.

Less than ten minutes passed as she walked to Winston's Flowers. Mya hadn't fully thought this next step through on her plan to reclaim happiness, but she only hesitated for a second before unceremoniously pushing her way into the shop. Bags and boxed easel clang against the glass door as she stepped inside. She had never noticed until recently how close she lived to

Winston's. How many times had she unconsciously walked past the small store before stepping into it for the first time late last year?

April was on the sales floor, a duster in hand, and she rushed to Mya's side, quickly relieving her of the box, placing it gently on the floor next to a display of roses in varying colors. "Hi, Ms. Monroe; it looks like you just robbed an art store!"

The girl was always sweet to Mya, and today, instead of a steely gaze of impatience, Mya actually gave her a small smile. "Nothing that daunting, I assure you. Is Luc..." she caught herself before using his first name, "is Mr. Gentry here by any chance?"

"In the back." She pointed towards the door Mya had now walked through several times over the last few months. "You can go back. Feel free to leave your bags here if you want. I can put them behind the register for you."

Mya called back over her shoulder as her feet began propelling her towards the door before her mind could catch up with her. "Thanks, April; I appreciate it."

Mya pushed through the door and found Lucas with his back to her. He had wireless earbuds pressed into his ears and was singing along to something she didn't recognize in a somewhat deep, gravelly tone. She paused, taking in his broad back, another flannel rolled up over strong forearms. Mya had never taken the time to actually study the man before, but now, even with just his back to her, she could see how beautiful he was.

His hands flew over piles of flowers on the large worktable, picking up stems and arranging them effortlessly into a large, white vase. Inserting sprigs of greenery to fill the space between buds and blooms, he manipulated them into gentle submission, each piece of his creation exactly where he wanted it to stand.

She wondered, as she silently observed him in his element, if his hands were as skilled in the bedroom as they were with the stems of exotic flowers, if he was as gentle with a woman as he was with the delicate stems, if his hands were soft or callused from work. Heat unfurled deep in her stomach as she thought about his large hands on her body, learning her curves and tracing them with his fingers.

About the same time Mya was struggling with the inner monologue of imagining Lucas in the bedroom, the hairs on the back of his neck stood on end. He had been fully focused on what was in front of him on the table, but took that moment to glance over the sink, where a mirror reflected a casually dressed Mya Monroe.

He studied her for a few seconds in the mirror-the curve of her heart-shaped face, lips still painted red but face devoid of makeup, her slightly ruffled hair, her rosy cheeks that looked like she had been working out.

Slowly, he turned to face her, pulling his earbuds from his ears and tossing them on the table.

"Mya." It was the only word to cross his lips, and it came out gruffer than he expected

She walked towards him, sliding a hand into her back pocket. Mya reached him in several long strides, and when she came to stand in front of him, she simply handed him the note, questions swirling in her two-toned hazel eyes. At the same time he studied the mixture of green and browns that radiated from her irises, she studied the vivid blue depths of his. It seemed like years passed as they unambiguously stared at each other, but in reality not more than a minute had passed.

He was handsome; there was no denying that. Mya found herself desperately searching his face, partly cataloging his features and partly for answers. When none came and he made no effort to speak, she uttered an almost silent, "When?"

Lucas brought a hand up to her face, gently placing it against her check. Uncharacteristically, Mya didn't flinch or pull away but almost unnoticeably leaned into the gesture. "When?" she repeated.

He let out a long sigh before dropping his hand, and they both noticed the strange loss of warmth.

"Your lips were still that gorgeous red, but your hair was longer. You had it up in a twist of some sort." He reached out, a lock of blue-black hair dancing between his fingers. "Your dress-" Lucas closed his eyes as if he were conjuring the memory in his mind," that fucking dress. Long, silver, covered in sequins." When he opened his eyes again, he stared straight into her, boring into her soul. "You were more fucking beautiful than the woman who walked down the aisle that day."

She cataloged her mind, searching for the time she wore the dress he was referring to. "The Diaz wedding?"

He nodded, almost solemnly, his eyes growing darker, almost royal blue. "The man you were with-Dave?"

It was her time to nod now.

"I watched before the ceremony started as he kept interrupting you when you were talking with a group of people. I watched how he held you back, I don't know if that was conscious or not, but he did. I watched the entire time, wanting to march up to you, to drag you out of that church, to kiss that sadness off your face, the same fucking sadness I saw when you walked into the shop the first time, the same fucking sadness I saw when you came in here drenched from the rain. Hell, the same sadness I saw last night at dinner."

April came into the back, breaking the spell between the two. "Lucas…" she looked between them, flashing regret for breaking the moment, "I'm super sorry, but I really need some help. The register is doing that thing again."

"I'll be right there." Mya expected him to be clipped with the young woman for interrupting, but instead, his tone was kind and familiar. Lucas turned to Mya. "Please wait here for me?"

His tone with Mya was different. Not stern, but commanding-dominant almost. It sent chills through her body, and she shivered despite the July heat that had seeped into the building through the open back door. She didn't think she could leave even if she wanted to, not with the way her mind and body were starting to operate separately from one another while around this man.

He exited the room leaving, Mya alone. She looked around for something to write with and found a yellow legal pad buried under the greenery on the table. She moved a few stems around until she found a pen and then sat on one of the stools, taping the pen against the paper a few times before scrawling a few words on the piece of paper. When she was finished, she ripped the page from the notebook and folded it in half before tucking it in her back pocket, unsure of what to do with it.

Mya spent a few minutes looking around, really admiring the flowers that almost surrounded the room. She wondered for a minute if any of these flowers were supposed to be used for her wedding but quickly pushed the thought out of her mind.

Her fingers were running along the velvety petals of a sunflower when Lucas reentered the back room. Standing behind her, he inhaled deeply, and while the scent of florals always hung heavily in the shop, he only smelled the sweet honeysuckle and jasmine that mixed together creating a scent that was intoxicatingly unique to this beautiful woman in front of him.

"Did you know that sunflowers are actually thousands of tiny flowers combined together?" She turned around to face him, and he pulled one of the thick stems from a vase and handed it to her. "Each petal that runs down to that center is surprisingly its own flower." His fingers caressed hers as they held the stem, and a sharp intake of breath filled her lungs. "Or that there are over seventy varieties of sunflowers alone? Some flowers are as small as six inches, some as large as two feet"

He kept talking, and Mya kept listening, staring in awe of the knowledge he held about something as simple as flowers. It was beautiful. "So many layers of petals, of individual flowers make up each sunflower as a whole. They remind me of you, actually. So many layers. So damn beautiful."

Mya's lips parted, and Lucas dropped his eyes to them before looking back into her eyes. He knew he couldn't push too much, too soon, but damn if he didn't want to devour her right now.

Still holding the flower, she reached into her pocket, pulling out the piece of paper she had tucked there for safe keeping. She held it out towards Lucas, and he took it, unfolding it and reading the text written in the center of the page.

Lucas,

Okay.

Yours,

Mya

He looked to Mya before dropping his eyes to the four sweetest words he ever read, and when he was sure he had read them correctly, he lost control. He grabbed Mya, turning her towards the nearest solid surface he could find-a walk-in cooler. He pressed her against it, slanting his mouth over hers. The most beautiful thing was that after only a second of hesitation, she kissed him back, her arms coming to tangle around his neck, sunflower still in hand. Their lips stayed locked, a more chaste kiss than either of them was expecting after the heat. Lucas finally broke their kiss, pulling her into a deep hug. He inhaled her hair, bringing his lips to the shell of her ear. Teasingly, he traced it with his tongue, causing her to shiver in his arms, before whispering lowly in her ear, "A month is never going to be long enough to devour you the way you deserve to be devoured."

Chapter Seven

While Lucas wanted nothing more than to keep his lips locked with Mya all day, he had to finish what he had started before her unexpected visit to the shop. But when he walked Mya back to the sales floor and saw the overflowing bags and box she moved to pick up, his dominant instincts took over.

"I'm escorting Ms. Monroe home," he spoke to the girl that Mya had grown to know as April. "Call Gwen and see if she can cover for the rest of the day. If not, shoot me a text, and I'll come back."

Mya started to protest but relented when Lucas fixed a firm gaze in her direction. Striding toward her, he effortlessly scooped the box under one arm, the other lifting the bags from the ground before stalking to the front door and exiting the shop into the bustling New York City street.

Less than a minute later, Mya joined him, coming to stand at his side.

"Lead the way," he gestured with the bags in his hand.

They walked in silence the few blocks to Mya's building, Mya nodding at the doorman who did a double-take when he saw her. She wasn't sure if it was because she was dressed so casually or because of the lumberjack of a man next to her, but for what was possibly the first time in her life, she honestly didn't care.

Fiddling in her purse, she procured the key card, swiping it against a panel in the private elevator car as the doors closed. As the car ascended floors, Lucas broke the silence. "You've lived in this building so close to me all this time, and we've never crossed paths."

Mya smiled, a shyness etched on her lips. "I was thinking that earlier, how many times I had uncon-sciously walked right in front of your store. Who knows?" She gave a noncommittal shrug. "We could have walked past each other hundreds of times…"

He cut her off before she could continue, that penetrating gaze locked with hers. "No. I would have noticed you."

A slight blush spread across her cheeks, and she

was only saved by the doors sliding open into the penthouse. Mya walked into the space, setting her purse on the entryway table, and for a moment, Lucas seemed glued to his spot. Only when she turned back to him did he step out into the foyer.

He let out a low whistle, his gaze sweeping over the open concept living and dining room before his eyes found the kitchen. "Woman, this place is next level batshit crazy."

She laughed, an actual laugh that spilled out from deep within her stomach. It was the first time Lucas had heard the sound, and it resonated within his soul as the sweetest fucking sound he had ever heard. He could die being suffocated by that sound and still die a happy man.

Mya broke his train of thought. "I suppose it is a little extravagant." She tried to keep a straight face, but she began laughing again.

He dropped the bags in the entryway, putting the box next to it. Lucas closed the short distance between them until there were only inches separating their bodies. "Did you…did you just make a joke, Ms. Monroe?"

"Maybe I did, Mr. Gentry."

He practically growled in response, walking her backward until her back was flush against the nearest wall. "You're mine for the next month, Mya. Unless you're on your knees calling me Sir, you will call me Lucas. No more of this Mr. Gentry bullshit."

Mya's pupils dilated until her eyes were almost completely black. Her breathing deepened as her chest rose and fell against his. She liked the slight dominance he showed, and even if she wanted to deny it, her body was a traitor, telling him exactly how she felt.

"And what happens if I continue to call you Mr. Gentry?" She wasn't sure why she continued to push, but not knowing what his reaction would be to her stubborn taunt exhilarated her.

Surprisingly, his voice deepened even further. "Do. Not. Test. Me. Mya." Lucas's words were staccato, and as he spoke them, he ran his nose from the base of Mya's neck to her earlobe, inhaling deeply as he did. He reveled in her feminine scent, a mixture of soft florals that transported him to the flower market he often browsed for inventory.

"Oh, but I'm learning it is fun, Mr. Gentry." Her eyes danced with defiance, her stubbornness turning him on even more than he already was. His dick had been half hard since the second he noticed Mya standing behind him at the flower shop, but now, he was rock hard to the point of pain. Lucas thrust forward, Mya still against the wall, and she gasped when she felt his hard length press against her body.

"Tell me right now, Mya. Are you serious about

doing things my way for an entire month? Are you ready to give yourself to me completely, relinquishing all control of your own body?"

One month, she thought to herself. One month with Lucas Gentry, and she'd know more about herself than she did in an eternity with Dave.

She didn't answer Lucas with words-simply nodded. It was slightly terrifying to her but equally as exhilarating.

"Then we're starting right fucking now, and you're going to learn not to call me Mr. Fucking Gentry ever again."

Lucas took a step backward, pulling Mya with him before lifting her effortlessly over his shoulder. He was walking through the penthouse, stalking towards a hallway before he spoke. "Where is your bedroom, Mya?"

"Last door on the left." As the breathy words left her mouth, Lucas picked up speed, not stopping until he pushed into the enormous suite. Mya did all she could to hold on for dear life, sending a silent prayer to the heavens that she would make it through this month unscathed.

Eyes scanning the room, Lucas took a moment to get his bearings on the space. A wrought iron, four-poster king bed jutted out from one wall covered with crisp white sheets. Of course, Lucas immediately fantasized about all the ways he could tie Mya to those posts, teasing her body until she unraveled under his touch. But that would have to wait until later.

He noticed the oversized abstract artwork that covered two walls in a splash of sage greens and dusty pinks. There was a chaise lounge and small table off to the side, and long curtains in the same sage green as the artwork framed stunning floor-to-ceiling windows. The chaise would do. For now.

Lucas dropped Mya to her feet before lowering himself to the chaise. He spread his legs wide, palming himself through his jeans while his eyes ran up and down Mya's body.

"Take off your clothes, Mya."

She suddenly felt very aware of herself. And of Lucas. Mya was turned on, as was evident by the painful little points of her nipples pressing against the thin fabric of her bra, by the heat pooling in her belly and wetness growing between her legs. Still, she was at once self-effacing, pulling her arms tightly across her midsection and diverting her gaze from the man who watched her with careful eyes.

"I'm only going to say it one more time, Mya. Take the clothes off your sexy fucking body. Fold them or leave them on the floor-fuck if I care-but you have one minute to take off your fucking clothes."

Lucas glanced at his watch as she stood, mouth

agape, feet glued to the plush rug that covered much of the wood floor. Mya wanted desperately to tear off her own clothing, but she was simultaneously enjoying pushing Lucas's buttons, eager to see just how far this little game of his was going to go.

"Forty-five seconds." He dropped his watch-clad wrist to the small table sitting next to the chaise, picking up a stray paperback book that looked out of place in the immaculately decorated room.

"Thirty." Lucas fingered through the book, arching a brow in Mya's direction when he stumbled upon what appeared to be a steamy sex scene where an apparent damsel in distress was getting rammed by three men. "Is this what you're into, Mya? You want three dicks to fill you at once?"

Her cheeks flushed, eyes darting from the novel he held back to his eyes. Did that idea excite her? Possibly. Would she ever act on such a fantasy? Absolutely not.

"Sorry to spoil your fantasy, baby. But I'm not the type of man who shares."

He tossed the book to the side, glancing at his watch again. "Fifteen seconds, Mya. You're really going to make me do this the hard way, aren't you, baby?"

She stayed motionless, staring straight ahead at him. She stayed in the same motionless stance as he counted down the final seconds as they ticked by on the secondhand of his watch. "Three, two, one."

Lucas sighed loudly, pushing himself upright. Standing now, directly in front of Mya, she had to crane her neck up to meet his lust-filled eyes. "I might be the friendly neighborhood flower shop guy to everyone out there," he gestured to the large windows and the city below them, "but in here-" he said pointing to the bed, "in here, I'm anything but friendly."

He lightly brushed his knuckles over her cheek before leaning down to kiss it gently. "Say sunflower, and it all stops."

Snaking an arm around Mya's midsection, he pushed her, face-first, onto the fabric of the chaise lounge with her feet still on the floor, taking care not to be too rough with her. Lucas mimicked her stance, his hard chest against her back. Mya felt his thick length press against her ass as he ran his hands down her sides, caressing the curves that ran from her hips up towards her breasts.

Without notice, Lucas righted himself, leaving Mya fully clothed but still feeling exposed. His large hand caressed her ass through her jeans, and she unconsciously gingerly leaned back into his palm. Lucas grunted in appreciation. "I was starting to think you didn't want this, but that little move you just did there baby, it tells me all I need to know."

Reaching down, he brought Mya upright, using the elastic of her bra for leverage before lowering his hand to her jeans, flicking open the top button with one smooth movement. He lowered the zipper painfully slow, the sound of the zipper's teeth almost echoing in the otherwise silent space. Lucas grazed a hand between the fabric of her jeans and cotton underwear, squeezing her ass hard, groaning in approval.

"Over two fucking years, Mya-over two fucking years, I've been dreaming of you, dreaming of having you. And I am going to have you, but right now, I'm gonna lay you over that pretty lounger of yours and smack your equally pretty ass until it's nice and red."

Lucas yanked her jeans down in one swift movement, causing a ragged gasp. She willingly stepped out of them as they cascaded to the ground, leaving her sandals and jeans in a pool at her feet. He took her hand in his, leading her over to the chaise. "Get on all fours."

She did as he instructed, and his already painful cock strained against his pants, begging for freedom.

He left on the rest of her clothes, her perfect tits hidden beneath the fabric of her shirt, her pretty little cunt he was dying to taste hidden from view with simple cotton panties. Lucas didn't know if her initial reluctance to undress was one of fear or defiance, but he didn't want to push his luck if it was the former.

"Mya, Mya, Mya." Her name was a tease on his lips, and he spoke it as he slid both hands over the perfectly round globes of her ass. "What do you say if you want me to stop, sweet girl?"

"Sun…sunflower." The word was but a mere whisper.

"Good girl, Mya. You're such a beautiful, good girl." He rubbed his palm over her ass once more before landing a smack on it, the resounding noise filling the room. Lucas caressed the cheek he had just smacked, leaning down to whisper in her ear, "I want nothing more than to pull those panties down your legs and slide my tongue between your legs." She audibly moaned as he slid a hand over her pussy, not penetrating the fabric that stood between them.

Mya wanted that too. She hadn't stopped thinking of that possibility since she woke up this morning and decided to put herself and her needs first. She knew Lucas Gentry would help her to do just that. She wanted to control her own life, and now, she was learning that in order to do that, she actually had to give up some of the control she was so used to.

"Do it." She spurred him on, slowly rocking back and forth against his palm.

A sinister laugh escaped his pursed lips. "Not today,

sweet girl. Today, I'm going to show you how good it can feel to wait, how good it can feel to be pushed to the edge, just close enough to fall but not close enough to plunge into oblivion. Have you ever given up control for even one day in your life, Mya?"

He didn't wait for an answer, just slowly continued to tease her with his fingers. His restraint was fading quickly, and if he didn't watch himself, he would lose control.

He wanted to lose control. God damn, did he want to. But as tempting as it was to slide his fingers inside her, Lucas abruptly removed his hand, instantly missing the heat radiating off her cunt.

Swiftly, he landed several more smacks over her ass, alternating between both her cheeks. Several times, he paused, massaging her ass cheeks, teasing Mya with a mixture of pain and pleasure.

"I bet if I pulled these panties down right now, your ass would be nice and red, wouldn't it, baby?" She moaned, almost a whine. "You're turned on, and I can tell. I can smell your arousal. You should see the sexy little wet spot growing against the fabric of your panties, Mya. It's the hottest fucking thing I've ever seen."

She should have been embarrassed that she was allowing someone to see her like this, embarrassed that she was on display, but she didn't care. Her body was on fire, and she wanted more, needed more from Lucas.

Mya dropped her body flush to the fabric of the chaise except for her ass which stayed high in the air. Her breathing had steadily increased since Lucas dared her to undress, and she decided to defy his request. Now, she was all but panting with wicked arousal.

Ever so slowly, Lucas lowered Mya's panties. He promised himself he wouldn't take them off, promised himself that he would remain in control. Her panties came to rest around her knees, and he let himself slide on a technicality that while they were around her knees, they were still on her body.

"Jesus Christ, Mya. You really have no fucking idea how gorgeous you are with your rosy ass on display for me."

She gave her ass a slow sway, back and forth, hypnotizing Lucas. "Just once," he groaned, more to himself than to her, before swiping a finger through her folds, her wetness coating his finger. The moan she released almost caused him to cum on the spot, right in his pants.

He reached around to her face, still pressed against the fabric, and brushed the finger over her lips, pleased when she darted her tongue out, licking her arousal from her full lips. "My perfect, beautiful girl."

Mya melted even further into the chair at his

praise. She never knew she would get off on being spanked, get off from being pushed to the brink of orgasm with a man's palm, but at this moment she felt totally uninhibited. And she liked the way it felt.

She hadn't finished the thought when the hardest of slaps landed against her now bare skin, and she yelped in response. It was quickly followed by another.

And another.

And another.

Each was harder than the last in a quickening succession. As he sped up, he started to rain slaps over her ass, alternating between light taps and fierce slaps that came with the flick of his wrist.

One last time, his palm connected with her skin, harder than all the rest.

"Lucas!" Mya yelled, breaking his spell.

All it took was that one word-his name spilling from her lips.

Lucas. Not Mr. Gentry.

Pulling Mya to her feet and then quickly into his arms, he carried her to her giant bed, laying her on the sheets with her panties still hanging from her limp legs. Lucas retreated to the edge of the bed for only a second, but it was an instant longer than Mya needed to think he was going to leave. Relief coursed through her body when she saw him return with a blanket, and she closed her eyes as he draped the blanket over her listless body.

Lucas removed his shirt before slowly climbing under the blanket next to her, pulling her into his arms. Mya's breathing was still ragged as if she had just finished a long distance-run, and Lucas instinctively wrapped her even tighter, knowing how difficult it was for her to be out of her comfort zone with a man she barely knew. "Beautiful girl." He gently kissed her lips. "Beautiful Mya."

Mya's hands came up to rest on his now bare chest, and with tentative hands, she ran long fingers softly over the light coating of hair that covered his muscular pecs. Her hands stilled but didn't retreat, and she found she liked the way his hard body felt against her curves, the way his even breaths matched hers as her breathing slowly returned to normal.

And although it was only mid-day and it had been years since Mya had taken a nap in the middle of the afternoon, she suddenly felt exhausted, tired from what had just transpired between her and the florist. Slowly, she felt herself drifting off to sleep, his strong arms enveloping her. And before she fully drifted off to sleep, she whispered his name once more, beginning to like the way it rolled off her tongue.

Chapter Eight

Mya woke in a daze, the afternoon rushing back to the forefront of her memory when she rolled and felt how tender her ass was. Wincing slightly, she glanced at the clock that adorned her nightstand. She gasped when the time read 7:03 P.M.

Sitting up slightly, Mya searched her mind, trying to think back to the last time she took a nap. She also couldn't remember the last time she woke feeling so entirely rested, and she relished in the feeling of calm that had miraculously overtaken her body.

Vaguely, she remembered falling asleep, a shirtless Lucas holding her close, lightly running his hands over her half-clothed body. Mya searched the room, a surprising sense of sadness clawing into her chest when she noted the bed next to her was now cold.

Her entire mood shifted.

He had left her.

Alone.

Somehow, this was always how she ended up-alone and feeling like she was utterly not enough. It had happened throughout her childhood, her parents often forgetting about piano recitals or awards programs at school. It had happened with Dave when she found him cheating on her. And of course, it had happened with her best friend who was on the other side of her now ex-fiancé's dick when she discovered their indiscretions.

But somehow, this hurt more.

Was she so unlovable, so unremarkable that she became disposable to everyone she let into her inner circle? Did Lucas leave because they didn't have sex? It hurt, even if he was the one who put that boundary between them.

Mya stood defeatedly, pulling a pair of yoga pants over her naked lower half. She scanned the room, eyes landing on a Jonathan Adler vase that was perched atop a tall dresser. One of her prized possessions, one side of the stoneware container had an almost animated sailor's face, his little head adorned with a nautical cap. The reverse side had a beautiful mermaid with intricate scales and long flowing hair, a crown of seashells furnished as a crown upon her head. It wasn't the most ornate piece of decor she owned, and when she thought about it, the piece didn't really even match her overall clean style. However, she had found the vase when shopping for a project a few years earlier and fell in love with the whimsy of it, bringing it home and happily putting it on display.

It had sat unused on her dresser since that day, but every time she looked at the vase, it made her smile. Looking at it now, she blinked several times, urging her eyes to come back into focus, for surely she was imagining things.

The mermaid was on display, and flowers spilled from the top of the vase. Mya walked to the dresser, marveling at the display that had almost appeared out of thin air. White roses, small daisies, and the tiniest sunflowers she had ever seen created a stunning bouquet. She couldn't help but lift it to her nose and deeply inhale the perfumed scent the flowers created.

"How…?" Her voice trailed off, her mouth suddenly going dry.

In search of water, she opened the door of her bedroom, slowly making her way towards the kitchen. Slowly, Mya noticed the soft sounds of Ella Fitzgerald that had filled the space. Coming around the corner of the hallway, she looked to the antique upright Victrola that stood against a wall, the top propped open, a record swirling under the needle.

Continuing to sweep her gaze over the space, her eyes came to rest on the man in her kitchen. Lucas, still shirtless, turned to look at her, as if he could instinctively feel her walk into the room despite the lack of sound she made. A wide grin spread across his face as he picked up a hand towel, wiping his hands off before crossing to Mya, pulling her into his arms.

"Hey there, sleepyhead." He ran a hand lightly through her hair, sending shivers over her body.

"I…" Her quiet voice cracked as she spoke, "I thought you left."

Stepping back from their embrace, Lucas searched her face, and while not completely sure, he thought he saw the shimmer of tears in her green-brown eyes along with definite pangs of fear.

Using a finger to tilt her chin up, he placed a soft kiss on her lips. "I took your key card from your purse and went out. But I never had any intention of staying away. Come; let me take care of you."

With six words, Mya felt the weight she had been carrying for as long as she could remember slowly start to evaporate.

"Let me take care of you."

Mya wasn't sure that anyone had ever said that to her before. She was minutely aware just how quickly she was becoming besotted with Lucas Gentry as he led her to the kitchen. He lightly tapped her rear before helping her to climb upon a tufted barstool at the sweeping kitchen island. He grew serious for a moment before speaking. "Are you feeling okay?"

Slowly nodding, Mya looked to Lucas, taking a moment to appreciate his impressively broad chest. Though he had laid in bed with her sans shirt, this was the first time she was able to really study him. And she liked what she saw. "Yes. Honestly," she confided, "I don't know the last time I felt so relaxed."

He smiled and placed a small kiss atop her head before continuing around the island, standing in front of a backdrop of fresh produce he had been in the process of chopping before she intruded. "I'll have dinner ready soon. Can I pour you a glass of wine?"

He spoke so confidently, not waiting for her to answer as he procured a second wine glass from a cabinet and poured her a glass. It was strange how at home he looked in Mya's space.

She took the glass he passed to her before turning his back, continuing to chop lettuce, carrots, tomatoes, and cucumbers. Looking at his toned back, she could see a faded tattoo over his right shoulder, the outline of several flowers. Mya smiled into her wine glass, thinking about how the tattoo suited him so well. Rugged on the exterior, but as she was quickly learning, so beautiful and nurturing on the inside.

"Do you cook often?" she asked, breaking the silence that had stretched between them.

He rummaged around a few cabinets, coming back with a large bowl. Sweeping the fresh vegetables into it, he turned and smiled at Mya, his eyes crinkling around the corners. "Only as often as I can. How about you?"

She laughed, that intoxicating laugh Lucas was becoming so incredibly fond of. "Does boxed spaghetti and jarred sauce count?"

He made a face of mock disgust, before laughing alongside Mya. "All this," he made a sweeping gesture to the kitchen, "and you don't like to cook?"

"Oh no, I like to cook, I am just absolutely inept when it comes to the kitchen. Once, I managed to catch toast on fire." Sheepishly, she brought her glass to her lips as if trying to hide behind the translucent glass.

A thunderous laugh erupted from Lucas. "How did you…?" He trailed off. "You know what, I don't even want to know. Also, I hope you're not a vegetarian or something like that."

"Oh no, I am absolutely a meat eater."

He laughed at her response and after thinking over

what she said for a split second, she was again laughing aside him. "Not like that, you crazed man!"

Continuing to laugh, he teasingly pushed her, earning a blush in response, "Oh, trust me, Mya, you will absolutely be eating my meat later."

Mya choked on the sip of wine she had just taken, almost sputtering the liquid all over the island. "Lucas! You can't say things like that when I have liquid in my mouth!"

He started to speak, but she cut him off. "Wait, don't even say it!"

Those soft lines appeared around his bemused yet vivid blue eyes as he stared at Mya, a huge toothy grin framed by his thick beard. "It's like you already know me so well, Sunflower."

Lucas reached out and lightly booped Mya on the nose-actually booped her on her small, upturned nose while she sat there, silently stunned by the silly little gesture. In the short time she had known Lucas, his attitude had always been slightly rough. Not impersonal, just absolutely not the nose booping type.

Turning back around to the food while Mya continued to stare at the mostly unknown stranger in front of her, he mixed a few ingredients in a small bowl and poured the mixture over the vegetables before doling out the salad. Placing one bowl in front of Mya, he walked around the corner, taking a stool next to her.

Lifting a forkful to her mouth, her eyes widened when she tasted the combination of flavors dancing over her tongue. Garlic, balsamic vinegar, even a hint of mustard played with her taste buds. "How did you manage to make a salad taste this good?"

He playfully bumped her shoulder with his. "You'll come to find that I'm full of surprises."

Turning to look at Lucas seriously, she spoke without an ounce of merriment in her tone. "I've begun to notice."

She returned to her salad, eating every last leaf of lettuce in the bowl while casually chatting with Lucas. It had initially startled her that she knew so little about Lucas, but now, talking with him in her kitchen felt so very natural. Mya was enjoying learning about him.

Walking around the island, Lucas plated two large helpings of tortellini carbonara before bringing them back to their seats. Both plates were balanced on one arm, a basket of warm rolls in the other hand. "I felt an ounce of guilt that you never got to enjoy your meal. It's not homemade pasta, but it'll do." He gave her a small wink.

Lucas reclaimed his seat, spearing a tortellini, and swirling it around in the rich cream sauce before lifting it to Mya's lips. Slowly, she parted them, allowing him to slide the tines into her mouth. She groaned, her entire body melting at the taste. Damn if Lucas didn't love the woman who made that noise.

Love. No, he quickly shook that idea from his brain. Lust, sure- a craving and desire to play her body like a perfectly tuned instrument. Abso-fucking-lutely. But love? He didn't know how to love. Or at least, he never allowed himself to love, too afraid of the repercussions.

Mya crashed through his thoughts. "Truthfully, how did you learn to cook like this?"

Lucas chose his words carefully, not wanting to reveal too much about his past. He hated the fake empathy that went along with his life story, hated the way people suddenly looked at him as less than when they learned that he had aged out of the foster care system and never had a real family like he was some sort of unloveable miscreant. It wasn't until he met his maternal grandparents when he was twenty-nine that he learned what family actually was.

"I worked in a few restaurants when I was younger. Starting as a dishwasher, I worked my way up to cook. One head chef sort of took me under his wing, and I learned most of what I know from him."

He left out the part about working under the table when he was as young as twelve, just looking to make a few dollars so he could eat while living with foster parents who only saw him as part of their family until they were blessed with a child of their own.

Here they were, two half-broken people who felt unlovable yet neither had the courage to tell the other exactly how their past had shaped them into the person that they were today.

She took another bite as she studied his words, a flicker of doubt crossing her features. "Well, Mr. Gen...Lucas," he chuckled at her almost slip up, "your hard work paid off. Feel free to cook for me every day for the next month."

His smile pressed into a thin line. "And what about after that?"

What the hell was he thinking, dropping lines like that? Like he actually believed that someone like her could find something worthwhile in someone like him to stick around for anything more than the short-term? She was wealthy, physically stunning, and mentally sharp. A woman like Mya would never be with someone like Lucas long term.

"Lucas," she sighed, pushing her plate away from herself, "today is only day one. Let's not get hasty. I could drive you crazy long before then."

His mood lightened, but by the lack of lines around his eyes, Mya could tell the smile was forced. "I don't think that could ever be possible."

She laughed though, a genuine laugh. "I think you underestimate me."

A long silence passed between them. "So, what happens now? Are you going to take me to bed and ravish me until I'm screaming your name?"

Suddenly, all pretense of Lucas remaining calm and steady left the space, his dick hardening at her words. His own voice came out lower, huskier. "Is that what you want, Mya? Is that all you want this month to be between us?"

"Yes," was her first word followed by, "no." She let out a frustrated half sigh half groan. "I...I don't know."

He didn't answer her, and she abruptly felt nervous under his scrutinous gaze, felt like she needed to keep talking when she just wanted to shut her mouth and stay silent. But her brain wasn't in charge right now, and the words came cascading from her mouth.

"I need to be honest with you and know that being open isn't the easiest thing for me." He regarded her words with a gravity, silently nodding at her to continue talking. "Dave, um, my ex-fiancé, well, he is the only man I've ever been with. I thought it was forever with him. Never strayed, although now I wonder how often he had. I just...I don't want to disappoint you." She trailed off as she ended her sentence, looking at him sheepishly before turning away, a slow embarrassment creeping up her cheeks.

Lucas pushed back from the bar, standing to his feet before turning Mya towards him. Gently, he used his thigh to push her legs apart until he could stand between her parted legs. She looked up into his eyes, seeing her reflection staring back in his deep blue irises. He was nowhere near ready to share his demons with this woman, but he would be damned if she showed this vulnerable side of herself to him and he didn't reassure her.

Tilting her chin up at the same time he lowered his head to hers, he captured her lips, kissing her once. He broke the kiss but kept his forehead pressed to hers. "You're a fucking remarkable woman, Mya. Zero men, one man, or a hundred fucking men, you could never disappoint me." Forcefully, he found her hand with his, placing it on his hard cock through the same jeans he wore earlier that day, guiding her hand back and forth against the fabric. "Does that feel like disappointment to you, baby? Because it sure as hell feels a lot like pure carnal need to me."

Mya gasped at the feel of his dick under her palm, but she suddenly realized she liked the way it felt. She wrapped her legs around his waist, hand still carefully placed under his, need coursing through her body as she pulled him closer.

"Then show me," she whispered in his ear. "Show me what pure carnal need feels like, Lucas."

"Jesus fuck, Mya." For a split second, she felt him grow even harder under her hand. But before she could react, she was thrown over his shoulder, for the second time that day, as Lucas stalked towards the bedroom, determined to show this woman exactly what pure fucking carnal need felt like.

Chapter Nine

Lucas had never been a pious man, but he was now a devout follower of the church of Mya. Laying her body down on her oversized plush bed as if it were a dais at which to worship, he started to slowly undress her.

Peeling Mya's top away first, he reached behind her back, unclasping the flimsy bra she wore that did little to hide her stiff little nipples. Lucas only took a few seconds to admire her perfect, pert breasts before sliding his hands down her sides, hooking his fingers into the elastic of her yoga pants.

"Hips up, beautiful girl."

Mya obliged, and Lucas slowly, so slowly that it was almost painful, pulled her pants down her long legs, discarding them on the floor when she was freed from the spandex prison.

He stood at the foot of the bed, his languid gaze taking in the goddess disguised as a mere mortal in front of him. As his eyes traveled her body, Mya's traveled his, and she was aware of how desperate she was to touch him. Trying to right herself on the mattress, she was met with a brick wall of Lucas's muscled chest when she lost her balance, hands planted firmly on either of his pecs. He responded with a small chuckle.

"Where are you trying to go, gorgeous?"

Mya's response came out breathy as she reached for the button on his jeans, and she was momentarily embarrassed when he placed his hands over hers, stilling her motion.

"I'm trying to get to you, Lucas."

He pulled her body to a standing position, her naked body flush against his. Trailing his fingertips lightly over her spine, she shivered, not from his touch, but from what he growled into her ear.

"Remember, Mya, I'm in control when we're in here. I say when you can touch me, when you can touch yourself, and even when you can come. And right now, I say that I'm finally going to taste that delectable cunt of yours before I command you to come on my tongue."

Her body was in the process of melting against his

when he spun her around, pulling her forcefully back against his chest. Strong hands traveled up her body, cupping her bare breasts. "God damnit, Mya, your tits were made for my palms." Lucas rolled her nipples between his fingers before pinching them.-hard. When Mya whimpered at the sensation, he did it again, and she responded by pressing her bare ass against his still-clothed cock.

One hand still on her breast, the other trailed down her stomach and over her hip before coming to rest on the smooth skin between Mya's legs. Lucas dipped his fingers between her folds, wetness covering his fingers, and they both moaned at the sensation. "Already so wet. So eager for me, aren't you?"

"God, yes," she rasped.

He rubbed small circles over her clit, the hand previously on her breast leaving her hot skin only to reappear around her neck like a collar. "Look at me, baby," he commanded, and Mya did without hesitation, her movement only slightly hindered by his hold. Pure, heated lust blazed in his blue eyes. "God, yes, is right," he groaned. "In here, I am your God, Mya." He speared her cunt with two fingers. "In here, I am your savior." He slid out before sliding back into her with three fingers. "In here, I am your fucking salvation."

Lucas tightened his grip around her neck, her eyes

widening while uncertainty spread across her features. Fingers still working deep inside her pussy, he walked them backward the few steps to the bed before releasing her neck, pushing her down onto the mattress, his fingers sliding free of her cunt.

Bringing his fingers to his own lips, he licked her wetness from them before stepping between her legs. "That look you gave me over there, that look of fear. Don't ever show that to me again." His voice wasn't angry but was cool and calm. "I might like it rough, but I'm not going to hurt you, Mya. I would *never* hurt you."

She nodded, her breathing heavy. "I trust you, Lucas."

A salacious smile spread over his face. "Good; now lay there like the good girl I know you are and let me fuck you with my tongue."

Lucas pulled Mya by her ankles to the edge of the bed, using his palms to spread her legs wider. Parting her sex with his fingers, he lowered his mouth to her cunt, sucking her clit into his mouth. A startled yelp from Mya filled the room, and she could have sworn that she felt Lucas grin against her pussy. Unhurried strokes of his tongue lapped between her folds as two fingers entered her. She could feel the scruff of his beard against her thighs and momentarily thought to herself that the sensation only added to the experience.

Curling his fingers upwards, Lucas found that secret sensitive spot, massaging it from deep inside.

Mya's hands fisted at the bedsheets as moans cascaded from her lips, already so close to the edge. "Lucas, please!"

He lifted his head long enough to speak before darting back between her legs, feasting like a man lost in the desert who had found the oasis that was Mya's taste. "Go ahead, baby; come on my lips, Mya."

Lucas sucked and licked and nipped at Mya's clit, fingers furiously thrusting inside her pussy. His other hand reached up, urging Mya to release hers from the sheet before linking his fingers with hers. He squeezed her hand once, letting her know he was still with her, and the small move of comfort in the middle of absolute bliss was enough to push Mya over the edge. Her eyes squeezed shut at the same time her pussy clenched around Lucas's fingers and pleasure coursed through her body. Spasms wracked her from head to toe as she came back to Earth and she nearly jumped off the bed when Lucas took one last long lick of her cunt.

Lucas settled on the bed, pulling Mya into his arms. He studied her features, now more relaxed than he had seen in the past, before leaning over to capture her mouth with his. Mya tasted the muskiness of herself on his lips and sighed into his mouth when she realized she liked the way the sweetness of his mouth mixed with her own flavor.

"Can I tell you something?" She asked the question with a tentative voice, shyness sneaking back into her tone.

Lucas nodded. "You can tell me anything, baby."

"That...I mean...I..." She stuttered her words, almost afraid to confess. "I've never done that before."

His head cocked down to look at Mya who wouldn't meet his gaze. "You mean you've never gotten off from someone licking your pussy before?"

"No, I mean, that's also true. But, I, um...I've never had someone go down on me before."

Lucas stared in amazement at just how innocent this sweet girl in front of him was in real life, his heart slowly growing in appreciation of just how magnificent she was.

Mya continued before he could speak, and while he wanted to interject, he also knew that this was something she needed to say. He could at least give her that safe space where she could open up to him. "My ex never wanted to." She motioned down towards herself. "He said it was dirty, unclean. So, while I wanted it, I just never pushed for it."

Lucas considered his words carefully before speaking. "You know that isn't true, right?" When she didn't speak, he continued. "I will spend every day of the rest of my life nestled between those sweet thighs of yours, Mya. I will fuck you with my tongue every day and worship your pussy the way you deserve it. And one day, you'll believe me when I say that it isn't fucking dirty but is the sweetest fucking taste to ever cross my lips."

Mya blushed before nuzzling her face into his neck, deeply inhaling his scent.

"How old are you, Mya?" Lucas's question broke the silence that stretched between them for several minutes. While he was marinating in the thoughts in his head, he realized there was still so much he didn't know about her. And he truly wanted to know everything when it came to Mya.

"Twenty-seven."

He murmured something incoherent against her hair. When he pulled back, he continued, now clear as day for Mya to hear. "You're so young and innocent, Mya. Such a beautiful girl." He stroked the side of her face tenderly. "I really am going to have fun teaching you that sex is something that should be enjoyed, not just done out of duty to a man."

Gaining confidence, Mya traced small circles over Lucas's chest with her long fingers. He had noticed the piano in the living room earlier, and while he continued to fantasize about those fingers exploring his body, he also found himself curious to know if she was the one who played the instrument. "Let's play a game."

Mya lifted her head to look Lucas in the eyes. "A game?"

He stilled her hand, pulling it to his lips to kiss her knuckles. "Yeah; I keep realizing there are so many things I want to know about you. Let's go question for question. I ask you one, then you ask me one."

She pulled a blanket up over her naked body and turned onto her side, head propped in her hand, eyes wide with amusement. "Okay, what burning questions are you simply *dying* to ask me?"

Lucas liked when Mya joked with him. He knew she put on a cool front to most and being on this side of the wall made him feel like she truly was going to give this month with him all she had. "The piano-do you play?"

"That's your question?" She raised a playful brow in his direction. "I do, or at least, I did. I don't play much anymore, but I took lessons from the time I was six until I was almost fifteen." Mya paused for a minute until it dawned on her that it was her turn to ask Lucas a question. "Um, how old are you?"

"I'll be forty-one next month." He expected her to balk when she found out about their age difference, but she just giggled.

"What's that laugh for, Sunflower?"

Mya liked the nickname, liked that Lucas compared her to something that was hundreds of moving parts that made up something beautiful.

"It's nothing." She shied away from Lucas, but he pulled her back to face him. "Okay, okay. It's just," she waved a hand in front of his bare chest, "I never knew forty-one could look so good."

He climbed on top of her, straddling either side of her torso, bringing his hands down to her sides and tickling her until she was squirming with laughter underneath him. "Are you calling me old, baby? Do you think I'm an old man, Mya?"

She could feel how hard he was against her but was unable to process his arousal. Mya was almost wheezing with laughter, rolling side to side to try to escape from under his weight, but he overpowered her in the best way possible. "Stop! No-oh my God, no!"

Lucas stopped tickling her but didn't climb off her body. Instead, he bent over her, pressing kisses to her lips, her eyelids, her cheeks, and her neck. "What's the deal with all the shit I carried back here today?"

"Painting supplies." She didn't supply Lucas with more information until he threatened to tickle her again. "Growing up, I loved to paint, but it was discouraged. I decided this morning that I wanted to work on putting myself first, making myself happy, and painting always used to do that. I'm hoping it still does the same."

"What else makes you happy?"

She tsked before poking Lucas in the side, causing him to jump slightly. "I thought this was a question for a question, sir."

Mya drew out the last word as if joking, but Lucas saw it as a dare.

He reached under the sheet with one hand, finding her still tender clit, and pressing two fingers to the bundle of nerves. Mya moaned in protest, but instead of lessening the pressure on her, he only added more. "Question for question is over now. You're playing a very dangerous game, baby. And when it comes to games, I always win."

Removing his hand from under the sheet, he brought both hands to his jeans, deftly unbuttoning the three buttons that ran down the front of his fly. His thick cock strained against his boxers, and Mya swore to God that she could feel herself salivating at the sight.

Palming himself through his boxers, his tone was again gruff. "Have you ever sucked a dick before, Mya?"

At a loss for words, she nodded, eyes darting between his cock and his eyes that had morphed into dark pools of the deepest ocean blue.

"Mmm…" He reached down, dragging his thumb over her lips. "But have you ever really sucked dick, beautiful girl, had a cock slide down your throat, struggling for breath as tears trickle from your eyes, your nose being held shut as you beg for air with your pretty hazel eyes, hot release jetting down your throat, and spit dribbling out of your pretty little mouth?"

"No." Mya's voice was hushed.

Lucas tugged his dick out from the slit of his boxers, precum already beading at the tip. "Would you like to experience that? And don't lie to me and tell me what you think I want to hear. Because I'll know if you do."

She gasped as she took in the full length of his rigid cock. "Yes."

With steady footing, Lucas stood on the bed, towering over Mya while removing his pants and boxers before settling back across her, his dick inches from her mouth. "Yes what, baby girl?"

"Sir. Yes, sir."

Lucas groaned at the words like he was hearing sound for the first time. Fisting his cock, he gave it several long, languid strokes. "Part those pretty lips for me, flower."

Heat flooded Mya's belly at Lucas's words. Her warm breath skimmed Lucas's dick as she opened her lips to give him access to her mouth, and he groaned in pleasure as he slowly pressed into her warm and wet mouth.

He punished Mya's mouth, didn't hold back, and Mya *loved* it, which surprised even herself. Part of her wondered if she would have always enjoyed being treated like this, like she was a toy for a man's pleasure. But no, she knew if Dave would have ever treated her like she was being treated at that moment, she would have been disgusted; she would have hated being treated the way Lucas was treating her now. Mya wasn't ready to admit it to herself, let alone to Lucas, but she knew the reason she was enjoying this was because of the man with his cock currently sliding down her throat.

Lying flat on her back, Mya was helpless under Lucas as he continued to thrust deep into her mouth. She gagged around his thickness, saliva dribbling from the corners of her lips as she struggled to swallow. He looked down, taking in her face before bringing his eyes to meet hers. Greens and browns swirled together around thick pupils, blown wide from lust.

"Mmm," he moaned. "You look so fucking sexy with my dick stuffed in your mouth, baby girl. The only thing that would make it better is if that pretty red lipstick of yours was smeared all over my cock and your face."

He stilled his movements, pausing with the hard

length of his most intimate part. "Breathe, Mya. Breathe."

She took in deep breaths through her nose, small tears slipping from her eyes, a whimper escaping out around him.

"Do you want me to stop?" She shook her head as best as she could.

"Do you want me to slow down? Be softer with you?"

Mya quickly thought about his words but dismissed them, shaking her head once again.

He growled with delight the second she shook that head full of raven hair, and without restraint, began to thrust again.

Over and over, he disciplined Mya's mouth as pressure built in the base of his spine. Lucas was close, so fucking close, as his dick slid in and out, mixing with the slippery spit collecting in Mya's mouth.

All he wanted to do, needed to do, was to explode down the back of her throat. He wanted nothing more than to feel her throat constrict around his cock as she drank down his hot cum.

"Baby," he gritted the word through clenched teeth, trying to hold on, trying to ride her face for as long as possible, to live in the bliss her perfectly pouty lips created, "I'm going to lose it if you keep that up."

Lucas began to retreat from Mya's mouth, but she

was overcome with a sense of bravery, a sense of need for Lucas-all of Lucas. Her hands, which had been gently resting on his thighs wrapped around him, taking hold of his ass. She pulled with what little strength she currently had, holding him inside her mouth while digging her meticulously manicured nails into his flesh.

And with that, with the mixture of her sharp nails against his bare ass and the hot, wet perfection that was Mya's mouth, he let go. His balls tensed before hot liquid coursed through his cock. His body stilled, and he grunted as he poured himself into Mya's throat. She drank him down, tears still spilling over onto her face before they traveled down to the twelve-hundred thread count pillowcase below her.

Slowly, he climbed off the angel beneath him, a content heaviness falling over his body. Lucas looked to Mya, the beautiful creature that had put her inhibitions aside to give herself to him. He was proud of her, proud of her for letting go, for pushing herself outside of the norm, for lying there next to him, looking absolutely nothing like the proper put-together New York City socialite she was.

He hoped his face conveyed his internal feelings, himself too afraid to speak them aloud. Instead of speaking, he reached out, pulling her close into his arms-skin against bare skin. He thought it was perfect-and right. And that everything was good in the world.

That was, it was perfect until Mya's body began to tremble next to him, gut-wrenching sobs cascading from her swollen lips.

Chapter Ten

ONCE THE TEARS started to flow, there was nothing Mya could do to stop them. A hurricane of emotions swirled through her suddenly exhausted body, her mind racing to try and sort through each. Facing Lucas, eyes squeezed tightly shut, she felt her body and breath trembling against his bare skin, but the contact did little to soothe the cyclone whirling within.

"Look at me, Mya," Lucas spoke softly, his voice gentler than usual but still just as commanding.

Still, she couldn't bring herself to open her eyes. Instead, she shook her head, using the minute ounce of energy she had left in her body to complete the simple task.

"Did I hurt you?"

She shook her head again.

"Are you okay?"

Eyes still closed, she managed an infinitesimal nod.

"Mya," his tone was still soft, but now, it was also serious, "did I scare you?"

Long seconds passed as small quakes continued coursing through Mya's body. Finally, she opened her eyes, searching Lucas's face, before she quietly responded, "No."

Lucas released a breath he didn't know he had been holding, a small sense of relief coursing through his body.

His arms tightened their hold around her as his hands lightly trailed over her spine. "I am so sorry, Mya. I should've known this would be too much, that you were gonna drop as soon as we were finished."

Although Mya was still emotionally and physically exhausted, her interest was piqued. She pushed back against Lucas until she could look into his eyes again, putting some much-needed space between their bodies. Even in her current state, she couldn't help but to be sucked into the swirling eyes that stared back at her. Stormier than his usual clear baby blues, Mya could have sworn she saw uncertainty in them now.

She spoke low and still hushed, unable to muster the energy for much more. "Going to drop? I don't understand."

"I'll explain it to you, Mya. But first, you have to let me take care of you. I'm going to get out of bed, but only to get you some water. Do you understand that?"

Mya's face didn't soften, but she nodded in agreement.

Lucas walked to the bathroom naked, toned features on display, and Mya hated that she couldn't even enjoy the moment. She didn't feel used-definitely felt sated, but there was something else she just couldn't put her finger on that was crawling under her skin.

The water turned on in the bathroom, breaking Mya's internal scrutiny of her feelings, and when she looked back to the doorway, Lucas was walking towards her, glass in hand.

Placing the glass on the nightstand, he gingerly helped Mya to a seated position before holding the glass to her lips. She took long gulps of the cool liquid, relishing the sensation of the water against her scratchy, used throat.

Lucas took the now empty glass from her hands before leaning into Mya, placing a chaste kiss against her swollen lips. "I'm gonna pick you up now, and I'm gonna to carry you to the bathroom."

She didn't move, didn't protest. At that moment, her body craved to be cared for-nurtured.

Mya allowed Lucas to scoop her from the mattress,

her arms coming to tightly wrap around his neck like a person overboard clinging to a life raft. He strode to the enormous tile tub that stood in the middle of the room. Water had already begun to fill the vessel, mixing with bath salts and bubbles, and Mya felt her body slightly relax when Lucas carefully lowered her into the warm tub.

Mya expected him to crawl into the tub with her, to push her forward and slide in behind her body. Instead, she was surprised when he pulled an oversized towel from a nearby rack, spread it on the tile floor, and sat next to the bathtub.

"You're overwhelmed." One hand reached over the edge of the tub, tucking a few stray strands of hair behind her ear. "You're so used to being in control, Mya." He sighed, searching his brain for a way to describe what she was feeling in terms that made sense. "Have you ever ridden a roller coaster before?"

"Yes."

"Well, you know when you're super psyched to ride one, and your adrenaline goes into fucking overdrive, pumping through your body? How you're excited and scared and maybe a little apprehensive all at once? How you wait in line until it is your turn, take caution in fastening the safety bar, and your heart begins to beat faster and faster as you make the climb up that first hill?"

Mya looked on, absorbing his words as he continued, "And how, when it's over, you feel torn between thanking God that the ride is over while your body begs to ride it again and again and again?"

He reached to Mya again, cupping her face with one large palm. "That's exactly what tonight was like for you, sweet girl. Your body has had so much adrenaline coursing through it, and right now, it's just not sure how to handle it."

She sat still for several minutes, smells of lavender permeating the air while the bubble-infused water floated around her body.

Mya mulled Lucas's words over in her head. In a way, it made sense. She had experienced that feeling, that drop as Lucas had called it, after completing big projects at work-riding the high and chasing the adrenaline rush of exceeding everyone's expectations, making sure every staging piece was in the perfect place, finishing ahead of the scheduled completion date.

When Mya started feeling that way at work, she would confide in Charlotte. The two women would grab drinks, celebrate the project, then binge on junk food and trashy television. It may not have been the healthiest coping mechanism, but it worked for Mya. Maybe she needed to treat this the same way? She decided that she would talk to Charlotte in the morning, hoping her friend could help her make sense of the entire situation.

Lucas broke the silence between them, a gentle hand coming to rest on her arm which had been draped over the side of the tub. "Are you feeling any better, sweet Mya?"

She did a mental scan of her body before answering truthfully. "Actually, I am.'

He gave her arm a light squeeze in response, drawing a small smile from her. "Come on, baby. Let me help you out of here, and we'll get you to bed."

Lucas had spanked her ass until it was red and angry. The same man's tongue had been lapping at her aching pussy just hours before. His cock had been forcefully shoved down her throat. She had confided in him about her sexual past and cried in his arms. Yet still, this was the moment she realized that she could fully trust him.

Helping her step out of the tub, Lucas tenderly patted her with a clean towel, wiping the wetness from her skin. The damp ends of Mya's hair skimmed across her shoulders, causing a chill to run over her body. When Lucas noticed, he pulled her in close, rubbing his hands up and down her body to bring warmth to her skin.

Moving to pick Mya up, she stopped him. "No, I can walk."

They locked eyes, and Lucas could sense her unspoken words. He didn't push the issue, although if he had it his way, the woman would never have to walk on her own again. He would carry her everywhere for the rest of his life if she allowed it.

He settled for continuing to nurture her through the unexpected emotions she had been experiencing. "Where are your pajamas?"

Mya pointed to the tall dresser as she took a seat on the bed. "Third drawer down."

Lucas moved gracefully for someone of his stature. Extracting a warm set of pajamas from the drawer, he returned to Mya and dressed her. "You seemed cold, so I thought these would be best."

Crawling under the sheets and turning to lay on her stomach, she sent a sly grin in his direction. "Well, maybe next time you'll flip the switch in the bathroom to turn on the floor warmer."

He laughed, the sound echoing from the walls and through Mya's body. Her smile widened as he playfully swatted at her behind. Slipping on his boxers, he climbed into bed with Mya. "Mmmm…I knew there was gonna be a next time."

She giggled as he continued, "And for real, you were holding out on me the entire time I was sitting on the cold-ass floor with nothing but a towel between my bare ass and the tile?"

"Excuse me, but from what I recall, I was in some sort of sex stupor and was unable to form coherent words at the time."

"It's called sub-drop, Mya. And believe it or not, it's very normal."

She searched her brain, trying to think where she had heard the term until it occurred to her that she had previously read it in one of her guilty pleasures; trashy romance novels. Instantly, pieces of the puzzle started to click in her head-Lucas demanding she call him "Sir," his use of the term sub-drop, the skilled way he used his hands against her skin.

"Are you…?" she trailed off, unable to push the words from her mouth.

Lucas wasn't the type of man to completely let her shy away, though. "Am I what, Mya?"

She huffed in exasperation, aware of exactly what he was doing to push her out of her comfort zone once again. "Are you a *dominant?*"

He seemed to consider his words carefully. "No, Mya, I am not a Dom like in those books of yours." He motioned to the chaise lounge where the book he had thumbed through earlier sat, and for the briefest of moments, Mya thought he was able to read her mind.

"Yes, I enjoy being more dominant in a relationship and very much enjoy a woman who is submissive. I like to be in control, and while I love nothing more than having you serve me, my only true end game is you receiving the most pleasure imaginable." His hand slid up Mya's back until it was casually resting loosely around the base of her neck. "I'm not into the scene, not looking to control you twenty-four hours a day, not looking to collar your pretty neck. I have no intention of sharing you with others or visiting specialty clubs where sex is openly performed. I simply want to fuck you every way imaginable, tease you in public from time to time, and maybe tie you up every once in a while."

Mya's mouth went instantly dry at the thought, and she unintentionally clenched her thighs tightly together as she thought about Lucas, rope in hand. That wasn't something she wanted from him, was it?

Again, it was as if he read her mind. "Stop thinking so hard, Sunflower."

Mya was still on her stomach. Lucas rolled her over, pulling her into his arms. "Tonight, we're going to sleep. You need to rest so you don't crash again in the morning."

Her body slightly tensed under his touch. "You're staying here tonight?"

"Do you want me to leave?"

"No. I was just expecting you to."

"Fuck, princess," he lightly chided. "I don't think

I've ever slept on sheets this soft. You couldn't kick me out if you tried."

Mya laughed a superficial laugh, trying to hide her doubts. Somehow, they always managed to leave, and she was sure that after the next month, Lucas Gentry would, too.

Chapter Eleven

Sitting across from Charlotte in a small corner booth, Mya was well on her way to being drunk. She had skipped work again, and although she had woken up tangled in a mess of sheets and limbs, she still woke with uncertainty deep within her belly.

Mya hurriedly pushed Lucas from her penthouse within minutes of him waking, brushing off his request to prepare breakfast for her. While she had felt better than the previous night, conflicted emotions still swirled through her head, and she knew she needed to work through them on her own. Well, at least on her own until she knew Charlotte would be awake. When she called, her friend eagerly agreed to meet her after work, and Mya knew that while Charlotte would absolutely help her to sort her thoughts, that her friend was equally as excited to drag out any sordid detail of the previous night that Mya would give her.

The girls had been giggling over appetizers and mixed drinks before moving to a strictly liquid desert as Mya had recounted the previous night's events. She told her friend *everything*-from the spanking, to how good it felt when Lucas went down on her, to how forceful he was when standing over her with his dick in her mouth. Charlotte sat in stunned silence, a rare feat for the woman. With her mouth agape, she twirled a lock of her long blonde hair around a finger as Mya described every detail.

Mya continued, replaying the myriad of emotions that had swirled through her body, how Lucas had reassured her and cared for her, how he helped her to relax with a hot bath, and how he still crawled into bed next to her and pulled her tight despite her freak out.

Her friend looked at her with stars in her eyes. "God, Mya, how the hell did you manage to have this dream man basically fall into your lap? Did he choke you? If you tell me he choked you, I might actually fight you for him."

Mya laughed, sputtering some of her drink onto the white tablecloth. "Oh, Lord, no!" The words came out louder than she expected, garnering annoyed looks from several other patrons.

The two broke into another fit of giggles as their server appeared, dropping off another round of decadent chocolate martinis. As she took the first sip, Mya's phone buzzed from within the small clutch she had placed next to her on the booth. Pulling it from the bag, she smiled as Lucas's name lit up the screen. "Well, speak of the devil."

"What's it say?!" Charlotte almost whined with excitement.

Mya slid her finger across the screen, tapping into the messaging app on her phone. "He says that he's thinking of me and that I should send him a picture."

Squealing with delight, Charlotte was next to Mya on her side of the booth in less time than it took Mya to blink. "Well, babe, let's give the hottie what he wants!"

Charlotte ran her fingers through the thick fringe of Mya's bangs, making sure she was camera-ready before taking the phone from her friend. Snuggling up next to Mya, she snapped a picture of them, giving the camera their most sultry looks. Staring at the picture, Mya laughed. "Oh, hell no, we're not sending him that!"

Her friend looked at the picture for several seconds before deleting the picture. "You're right, we can make this better. Grab your glass."

Mya complied, taking her glass from the table.

Charlotte, sassy woman she was, reached over to her friend, pulling the top of Mya's dress down to show off an almost obscene amount of her cleavage. The two women nuzzled closely, Charlotte making duck lips at the camera as Mya threw her head back and laughed, drink still in hand.

Before Mya could process what was happening, Charlotte snapped the picture, sent it to Lucas, and handed Mya her phone back. "Sorry, babe, I knew you would have chickened out."

Mya didn't have time to protest her friend's actions before her phone buzzed again.

Lucas: **Mya, how much have you had to drink tonight?**

Mya: **Not enough to stop thinking that we're doing something we shouldn't be doing.**

She tossed her phone back into her clutch before returning her attention to Charlotte, who had moved back to her side of the table and her chocolate martini.

Lucas had recognized the bar the second the picture came through on his phone. Well, the second he was able to tear his eyes from Mya's tits in what looked to be a super tight black dress.

Twenty minutes later, he was entering through the door to Luxe, his eyes scanning the dimly lit bar. His gaze heated when he found Mya, sitting in a booth near the rear of the lounge with her back to him. He would know the slope of her neck anywhere.

Two men stood at the end of the table, trying to engage the women in conversation, and it made Lucas's blood boil. He took several long strides across the bar area, becoming angrier with each step. Nearly losing his shit when he heard Mya giggle at something one of the men said, he simply walked to the table, excused himself to get by the man, and took a seat in the small booth next to Mya.

"Gentleman," he looked to the men, his voice dripping with snarl, "thank you for keeping my woman company. You can go now."

He didn't look at the men, simply kept his gaze glued to Mya who sat in shock, her lips slightly parted.

Charlotte's eyes darted between Mya and Lucas as the two men quickly retreated to the bar. "Um, I suddenly have to use the little girls' room," she squealed, her voice even higher than normal. Mya finally broke the trance Lucas was holding her under, looking to her friend. Charlotte silently mouthed "You okay?" When Mya gave her a small nod, Charlotte stood, grabbed her handbag, and darted towards the bathroom.

Returning her attention to Lucas, she opened her mouth to speak but couldn't get words out before he cut her off.

Growling into her ear, his voice held an edge of danger. "I should take you over my knee right here Mya, pull up that tight little dress and mark your ass with my hand to make not only you, but everyone else in this bar see that you belong to me."

His hand was on her thigh, squeezing tightly. Mya's words were breathy when she responded. "How did you know where to find me?"

Releasing his hold on her thigh, he trailed his fingers under the hem of her short dress, causing her to squirm. "Sweet girl, you forget that we live in the same neighborhood."

In all honesty, Mya hadn't thought about where Lucas lived. She knew that her penthouse and the flower shop were close to one another, but she didn't know that he also lived in the neighborhood.

He took Mya's martini from the table, downing the rest of the liquid from the chilled glass. Placing it back in front of her, he took the same hand that had been holding the glass and used it to turn Mya's chin. "You know seven A.M. comes early, Mya. And you and I have a busy day ahead of us tomorrow. You better not be late."

Charlotte reappeared at that moment, sliding back into the booth opposite her friend. "Well, hello there, lovebirds. Can I get either of you a drink?"

Mya grimaced at her friend.

"I was just leaving," Lucas said, his voice still low. He leaned into Mya, snaking one hand into her hair to turn her face towards him. Not waiting for permission, he kissed Mya, parting her lips with his tongue to enter the wet heat of her mouth.

His other hand, still under the hem of her dress, ran up between her thighs, and she gasped into his mouth when he dipped under the fabric of her panties, taking one swipe through her delicious cunt.

Lucas slid his hand from between her legs at the same time he released his hold from within her tresses. Pushing up from the booth, he looked at the stunned blonde across the booth before turning back to Mya. "See you in the morning, Sunflower."

Mya sat in stunned silence. Her fingers coming up to touch her lips, still wet from Lucas's tongue.

"Jesus Christ," Charlotte hissed through gritted teeth. "That was seriously the hottest fucking thing I've ever seen!"

A small smile spread across Mya's face. She knew her friend couldn't see what had happened under the table, but that kiss? That kiss was enough to send shivers over her body. Breathlessly, she replied, "Yeah, it was."

Charlotte looked across the lounge, flagging down their server. "Well, what the fuck are you waiting for! Go get that sexy florist! I'm paid surprisingly well; I've got this."

Mya stood, grabbing her clutch, unable to believe that she was about to chase after Lucas Gentry. "I've got next time, Char!"

Less than a minute after Lucas left the bar, Mya burst through the doors into the hot summer night. Lights illuminated the street, people's chatter drifted in the air, and cabs honked in the distance. Left, then right, her head snapped, searching for Lucas.

Her stomach dropped when she didn't see him. Unaware of which way he would have gone, she was about to turn around and admit defeat, about to walk back into the bar and drown herself with even more alcohol.

Lifting her head, she took one glance across the street, her eyes locking with Lucas's deep blue gaze as he stood propped against a light post. Mya's breath hitched, her chest rising and falling heavily. Taking a quick glance across the street, she hurriedly crossed when the traffic had cleared, not stopping until she stood directly in front of him.

Uncharacteristically, she pushed up on her toes, heels slipping from her narrow-heeled shoes. Bringing her arms around Lucas's neck, she pressed her lips to his.

While her kiss was chaste, Lucas overtook her with passion quickly. Parting his lips, he allowed her to tentatively explore his mouth first, giving her the control she thrived on before not-so-gently reminding her that she belonged to him for the next month. His hands were in her hair while hers were on his broad chest. Mya could taste the lingering chocolate on his tongue mixed with a hint of butterscotch and she groaned against his mouth, as he smiled into her kiss.

Lucas captured her bottom lip between his teeth, biting hard enough for a small yelp to escape Mya. "You're a very dangerous woman, Mya."

She was breathless, unexpected need coursing through her system. "No. You're the dangerous one. And I think I'm ready for you to show me just how dangerous you can be."

"Mya..." His voice was low and gritty, fueled by his own need.

She stopped his words with another kiss, her hand slowly working lower and lower down his chest. "Take me home, Lucas. Show me how good it feels to lose control."

He stopped her hand from traveling any further,

grasping her wrist tightly. Searching her eyes, he could see the need, the lust. And damn if he didn't feel it, too. Starting to walk, he pulled her behind, her tiny feet working double-time to keep up with his long strides.

"My penthouse is in the other direction."

Lucas didn't stop, simply kept walking, both sets of their feet sending echoes off the New York City sidewalk. "We're not going to your penthouse. You're coming home with me, Mya."

They walked in silence for a few minutes until they stood in front of Winston's. Mya stared straight ahead as confusion marred her beautiful features. "What are we doing at the shop?"

Lucas pulled a key from his pocket, unlocking a door to the right of the shop front. Holding the door open for Mya, he ushered her up the narrow staircase into an open loft.

Exposed brick walls outlined beautiful, large windows. A small kitchen was off to the far right, and oversized leather couches were covered with a few neutral throw blankets and patterned pillows in the living space. To the left, a staircase led to what Mya presumed was a bedroom.

"It's not the penthouse, but it will do."

She briefly thought she heard a lack of confidence in his tone, but she liked the space immediately.

"No, it's perfect." Mya walked to the windows, the corners of her lips turning up into a smile when she saw that Lucas even had fresh flowers in his decidedly masculine space. She could just make out a sliver of Central Park through the windows and noticed that a small balcony jutted from the side of the building.

He came to stand behind her, wrapping his arms around her waist and kissing her on the top of her head. "It's perfect with you here, Mya. You're perfect. You make everything brighter just by being in this world."

Twisting in his arms, she stood to face him. Emotion swirling in her eyes-need and lust, but also pain and longing. "Show me, then. Take me to bed, Lucas. Show me how perfect I am."

Chapter Twelve

BARELY TWO DAYS with Lucas Gentry and Mya was growing accustomed to being tossed over his shoulder. This time, he was climbing the stairs to his lofted bedroom, two at a time, while acting like Mya weighed about the same as a bag of sugar.

Mya bounced ungracefully as Lucas tossed her to the bed, coming to land flat on her back with her legs hanging off the edge. Finding amusement in her precarious position, Lucas laughed as he walked to his end table, switching on a lamp. Dim light filtered across the room, casting an amber hue across Lucas's profile. Mya spent a few long seconds taking in his sharp features before he turned his gaze back to hers.

Any trace of his previous amusement faded,

replaced by pure desire. Pupils dilated, he watched Mya as if he were a lion on the Serengeti, poised for attack. Lucas closed the distance between them, easily pulling her into a seated position. He pushed her legs as wide as they would go while still covered in the tight sheath dress, stepping between her thighs while tilting her chin up with a finger.

"Sweet, beautiful Mya. You have no idea what you do to me."

Her breathing became labored as his hand slid from her chin, up her cheek, and tangled into her inky black hair. "Tell me."

With a growl, he tightened his hold on her tresses, leaning down to gruffly speak into her ear. "You make me want to be a bad, bad man, Mya. I want to maim any other man who dares to look at you. I want to tie you to this fucking bed and use your body for not only your pleasure but for my own greedy need. I would harm anyone you wanted me to, fucking kill anyone you asked me to, if it meant there was a fucking chance that you would need me in the desperate way I need you."

Chills broke out across Mya's body as heat pooled deep in her belly, each temperature begging to overtake the other. She had never felt this pull to someone before-felt this raw, lascivious need to be consumed. She yelped as Lucas pulled her to her feet, fist still wrapped in her hair, and tears threatened to prick at the back of her eyes at the sensation. There was a small part of Mya that wanted to run, to get as far away from Lucas as she could. But even more than wanting to run, she wanted to succumb to whatever delicious torture Lucas had planned for her.

Pupils blown wide from her own desire, she was nearly breathless as she mewled, trying to escape Lucas's tight grasp.

This was not Mya. She was poised, always in control with an icy-cool demeanor. But where had that gotten her in life? She was supposed to be walking down the aisle in less than twelve hours, her failed engagement looming heavily over her head. Mya had never been the type to have many friends; she found most people didn't take kindly to her demanding personality. Hell, thinking back over her life, she barely ever even had the support of her parents. They treated her more like a possession than an actual human.

"Hey there, Sunflower. Care to share any of those thoughts with me?"

Afraid that anything she would say would break her from the trance she was under, she pushed the intrusive thoughts down, determined to focus on the man in front of her. She wanted to feel all the words Lucas had spoken to her moments ago, wanted to feel so incredibly desired that it consumed her and set her body aflame.

Still afraid to speak, she simply reached her arm behind her back, unzipping her dress. Lucas stilled as she slipped the thin straps down her arms, allowing the dress to fall to the ground, pooling at her feet.

He finally released his grip on her hair, taking a step back to admire her body, now clad in nothing but a lacy black bra and matching thong. Walking a slow circle around her, Lucas leisurely drank in her body, a low growl of appreciation rumbling from his throat. "I'd burn the fucking world down if it meant I got to look at you like this every day for the rest of my life."

Lucas trailed a finger down her spine, goosebumps breaking out over Mya's flesh. He dipped a finger beneath the lace of her panties, ripping the scrap of cloth off her body with one swift movement. She gasped as it fell to the ground, her hand instinctively trying-and failing-to cover up the most intimate part of her body.

Taking her delicate hand in his, he dropped it to her side, giving himself an unobstructed view. "Don't you dare hide yourself from me, baby, and don't you *dare* be afraid of me."

Standing in front of Lucas, she was afraid. But not of him. Mya was afraid of her own insecurities, ashamed that she had let so many other people dictate her life until this moment. She took a deep breath, her steely gaze locking on Lucas. Speaking aloud, the words were just as much for herself as they were for him. "You don't scare me, *Sir.*"

If Lucas's dick was hard before, he turned into absolute steel when he heard Mya breathlessly call him Sir. His lips were on hers in record time, fingers tangling in her hair. Mya moaned into his mouth, and he deepened their kiss in response. Her hands came up to his chest, nails lightly grazing over his muscles. She loved the way his broad chest felt under her hands, the light smattering of his chest hair tickling her fingers as she explored the ridges and grooves of his chest.

Abruptly, he stepped back, reaching for the buckle on his belt. Fingers working the metal, he made quick work of ridding himself of the leather, holding it loosely in one hand. "Hands behind your back, beautiful."

Mind reeling, Mya complied before she could talk herself out of it, bringing her hands behind her back. Lucas looked at her, a mixture of pride and desire flooding his darker-than-normal features.

"Such a good girl."

Lucas reclaimed his place behind Mya, belt still in hand. He trailed kisses over her shoulder blades, and she squirmed at the feel of his bristly beard against her smooth skin. Chuckling in response, he leaned into her ear. "You like that, Sunflower?"

Moving her lips to answer, she managed to moan a singular, *"yes"* at the exact same time Lucas gently bit down on the top of her shoulder. The sensation ricocheted through her body, the roughness of his bite paired with the extreme softness of his lips kissing her skin was the perfect contradiction.

"So help me, God, if you leave a mark on me, Lucas-"

He laughed while bringing her arms closer to each other, still behind her back. Looping his belt around her wrists several times, he tucked the end between the leather, making sure it wasn't too tight against her skin.

"Sweet, sweet Mya. I thought we already established that in this room, I am your God."

Lucas pulled on her restrained wrists until she was flush against his chest. One hand held her in place while the other snaked from the column of her neck down the front of her lithe body. Teasing her nipples through the fabric of her lacy bra, the already sensitive bundles of nerves became almost painful under his hand as he alternated between light touches and rougher pinches. She whimpered, trying to create space between his hand and her breasts. Lucas didn't care. Tonight, he wanted to hear her beg, wanted to hear his name spill from her pouty lips again and again and again.

"Trying to get away from me already?"

Her body was overwhelmed with sensation, and he hadn't even moved his hands from her nipples. "Yes… no…I don't…" She found herself unable to speak any further as his hand left her breasts, trailing down the flat plane of her stomach.

"Always tell me the truth, baby girl." He lightly trailed his fingers across her hip. "If you ever want me to stop, need me to stop, just say so." She dropped her head to the side as he dipped one finger between her legs. Nipping at her neck, he continued, "This is all about trust. If you can't put your trust in me, then you should walk away right now."

"Lucas," his name was nothing but a breathy pant, yet he stilled the hand he had been exploring Mya's body with, waiting for her confirmation to move forward. She couldn't look into his eyes, her back still to his chest. She slowly bucked her hips into him, urging him for more, "I trust you."

With those three simple words, Lucas's control broke. Spinning Mya to face him, he grabbed her chin with one large hand, lips crashing into hers. "Your lips are the sweetest fucking thing I've ever tasted."

Walking her back to the wall, he only stopped when they had nowhere else to go. With just enough space to reach his hand between their bodies, he quickly unzipped his jeans, pushing them down just enough that he could free his cock from the denim.

Lucas pulled a condom from his wallet and presented the foil packet to Mya. He gingerly traced her lip with the rough edge of the packet before urging her to open her lips. Mouth slightly parted, he placed the wrapper in her mouth before instructing her to open it with her teeth. He pulled the wrapper, allowing a small tear to form in its exterior, and when he could free the condom from within, he let the wrapper fall to the floor between them.

Expertly rolling the condom over his thick shaft, he spoke to Mya without reservation. "One day, I'm going to fuck your pussy raw-nothing between us. I'm gonna fill you with so much cum that it leaks out of your cunt. And when it does, I'm going to wipe it from your pussy and make you lick it from my fingers."

Eyes wide, she was taken aback by his raw honesty and found that his words made her even wetter than she could ever imagine. It gave her confidence to hear him say such filthy things to her, knowing that he absolutely meant each word. Mya wanted to be more like Lucas, wanted to liberate herself from inhibition and simply live in the moment.

She decided she could start right then. Looking at

Lucas, hunger blazing in his eyes, her voice came out dripping with need. "Fuck me, Lucas."

A growl tore from his throat as he picked her up. Instinctively, Mya wrapped her legs around his waist, steadying herself against the sturdy wall behind her. Lucas lowered her down onto his waiting dick, working his length inside her inch by agonizing inch. She already felt so full, so claimed, that she nearly passed out when he murmured against her ear, telling her that she was halfway there. "I can't do it; I can't take all of you."

"You can and you will, sweet girl." He momentarily lifted her up before lowering her, sinking deeper into her pussy. A pathetic mewl fell from her lips as she worked to accommodate his size. "You're doing so good, Mya-so, so good."

His dick sank even further into her until she was fully seated on his length. Stilling, she took several deep breaths, his quiet affirmations breaking into her own silent meditation. "Look how good you look sitting on my dick. You look so beautiful, cheeks all flush, tiny little beads of perspiration clinging to your neck." Lucas bent into her, running his tongue down the slope of her neck.

With agonizing slowness, he began to thrust into Mya while simultaneously lifting her up and down. While part of Lucas continued his slow pace to make sure Mya could take him, he also selfishly knew if he started to truly thrust into her cunt, that he would blow like a middle schooler seeing a tit for the first time.

Arms still tied behind her, she could do nothing to control the pace. Utterly helpless against his slow ministrations, she needed more, wanted to feel him even deeper. Lucas could read her, knew she wanted something but was too afraid to ask-too reserved.

Continuing to slowly move in and out, his arms still firmly planted on her hips, he leaned in close, whispering in her ear, "Tell me what you want, baby. Tell me what you need because I want to see you come undone, and I want to be the reason you do."

"More. Faster." Mya wanted to be able to touch him, to run her hands through his hair, to scratch his skin. She settled for capturing his bottom lip between her teeth, gently biting his lip before releasing it. "Faster," she repeated again.

"Keep those legs wrapped around my waist, baby."

Without warning, he lifted her fully off his cock before sinking her back down in one harsh movement. She was wet-soaked. But the sensation still caused her to scream into the silent room.

Lucas's hips sped up, his forearms burning as he held onto her hips, bruising the skin underneath his fingers. "You want faster, baby? You want harder?"

Mya nodded as he started to furiously fuck her.

Grunts and moans and the smell of their sex filled the room around them. Still, it wasn't enough.

It wasn't enough until Lucas, as if reading her mind, pulled her away from the wall, carrying her to the bed before depositing her on the mattress, ass in the air. Face to the mattress and arms still behind her back, she was now on full display for Lucas. And the thought excited her.

Lucas laid one strong smack across her ass before burying himself back inside her cunt from behind. "Damnit, Sunflower. Your cunt is so tight around my dick."

His pace was relentless now, his only desire to make her cum. Hips pistoning over and over, he thrust into her while snaking a hand around her body, two fingers rubbing her clit.

"Ahhh…!" The sound came from Mya, though it sounded alien to her own ears. She was racing towards bliss, so close to toppling over the edge, and sure she was having an out-of-body experience. "Don't stop, Lucas. Please, don't stop!"

He had been holding himself off since his dick had its first taste of Mya's cunt, thankful that she was close. Determined not to cum until she did, his thrusts were punishing as he slammed into her over and over and over.

One hand still working over her clit, he pulled her

towards him with the other, using her belted wrists to raise her off the bed. Now on her knees, he was still inside her, still pushing them both towards climax.

Lucas wrapped his hand lightly around Mya's neck, more to hold her in place than to show her how heightened the experience could be with her air supply obstructed. "One day, beautiful girl, I'm going to tighten my grip on your neck while I'm inside you. I'm going to bring you even closer to God than you are right now."

With those words, her muscles clenched around his cock as her entire body tingled. She wanted it. And there was no doubt in her mind that someday, she would let him.

Mya's orgasm coursed through her body, white spots dotting her vision, a guttural scream echoing in the space around their bodies. Lucas was right there with her, so close to falling over the precipice into oblivion, falling past the point of no return as his name came spilling from Mya's lips.

His hips stilled as he poured his seed into the condom, wishing he was painting the inside of Mya's walls with his cum instead. Holding Mya to his chest as spasms wracked through her body, he slowly pulled from her pussy, missing the heat the second he was out.

Gently, he lowered her to the bed. As she lay on her side, he removed the condom, tying it off and tossing it into a trashcan next to the bed. Carefully, he untied his belt that had been used to bound her wrists, brought her wrists between them, and gently rubbed them, bringing feeling back into her extremities.

Her eyes closed, a relaxed, blissed-out look encapsulated her facial features. Still, he knew what happened the last time they were intimate, and small tendrils of doubt made him speak up before she fell asleep. "Sunflower, check in with me."

She looked at him confused.

"Tell me that you're okay."

She smiled a genuine smile, her perfectly white, straight teeth on display. "I could get used to that."

He laughed in response, pulling her closer, strong forearms wrapping around her body. "Me, too, Mya. Me. Fucking. Too."

Chapter Thirteen

SCANNING HER SURROUNDINGS, Mya was momentarily confused when she awoke on Saturday morning to the sound of an alarm clock that was not her own. Stretching her limbs, she found a snoring beast of a man in bed next to her, seemingly unphased by the blare of the alarm.

Climbing from the bed, she pulled down on the t-shirt Lucas had given her to sleep in before lightly padding across the room to silence the alarm. Looking back to the bed, she took time to study Lucas's features as he slept, and for the first time, she really studied the gorgeous man. His features were softer in his current state, the creases around his eyes less prominent-a stark contrast to the man who often looked like he was carrying the weight of the world on his broad shoulders. She thought she saw just a hint of gray in his thick beard, and on closer inspection, she saw the tiniest little scar on his nose that looked like it may have been caused by a once-had nose piercing.

Mya's eyes trailed down his body, clad only in black boxer briefs while being free of the light blankets they had slept under the previous night. Corded forearms, the sexiest forearms she had ever seen, swept up to toned biceps. Sculpted shoulders and defined abs proved that the man worked out, and Mya wondered if that is why he appeared to look younger than his forty-one years. She was staring at his calves, impressive even while relaxed, and trying to make out the faded tattoo under the coarse hair coating his legs.

Thoughts strayed to her ex-fiancé and just how different the two men were from one another. Dave had been the same age as Mya with sandy blonde hair and green eyes, a stark contrast to Lucas's almost black hair and bright blues. He wasn't exactly soft around the middle, but not toned and defined like Lucas either. She liked how Lucas towered over her, having to be at least six foot five inches while Dave had stood almost eye-level with her.

For as long as she could remember, she and Dave had simply existed within the same space while she found she actually enjoyed spending time with Lucas.

She liked his gentle teasing and his rough hands, his sweet nicknames and dirty words whispered only for her to hear.

Upon waking, she expected her heart would have been in a million pieces as she thought about the wedding that was supposed to happen that morning, but instead, she found herself content in an unexpected way.

"Enjoying the view, Sunflower?"

His voice was soft, dripping with sleep, but the unexpected intrusion to Mya's thoughts was enough to make her jump, her heart leaping into her throat. "Shit, Lucas. You scared me!"

Pushing himself into a seated position, he pulled Mya into his arms while quietly laughing. "Sorry, baby."

With her still wrapped in his arms, he took an inconspicuous inhale of her hair. Lucas worked with the most beautifully fragranced flowers every day, yet he already believed that Mya smelled sweeter than any flower ever could. Notes of jasmine mixed with citrus complemented by just a hint of eucalyptus blended with the scent of sex that still hung heavy in the air. "We've gotta get downstairs, but if I can manage to let go of you for five seconds, we should have time for a quick shower."

"But I don't have anything to wear. I need to get home and change."

Standing like she was getting ready to leave, Lucas pulled on the hem of the shirt she was wearing. "I don't know; you look pretty good in this to me."

Mya's cheeks flushed pink. "Lucas, I don't even have underwear since you so graciously tore mine from my body last night."

A salacious grin spread wide across his face in response. "Are you complaining?"

She didn't answer, just stared at him dumbfounded until he spoke again. "Come shower with me. You can throw on a pair of my sweats to work in the store with me, and then we'll swing by your apartment and grab clean clothes before we make our deliveries. I'm sure April has some flip-flops or something downstairs that will fit you."

Knowing it was a battle she wouldn't win, she relented before following Lucas to the bathroom.

His primary bathroom was larger than she would have expected, the entire space designed to accommodate water. A rainfall shower stood in the middle of the room, several overhead showerheads mounted from the ceiling. There was an oversized tub that looked like it had never been used, and a floating double vanity that contained dual sinks and mirrors. It came as no surprise to Mya that there were even signs of life in his bathroom, though here, instead of flowers, the shelves held plants of varying sizes and shapes.

Absently dragging her finger over the smooth edge of the counter, she took in the space with the part of her brain she reserved for interior design. "This is not what I was expecting. Actually, it's beautiful."

Turning on the showerheads, Lucas shimmied out of his boxer briefs, smirking when he saw Mya's gaze momentarily slip to his half-hard dick. "Sorry, Ms. Penthouse, but there are no heated floors here."

She laughed in response, hesitant for only a moment before lifting the shirt she had slept in up and over her head. Walking under the hot water where Lucas already stood, he groaned, gesturing to his now fully erect cock. "Do you see what you do to me?"

Mya stepped back, putting space between their bodies. "Oh, no, smooth guy. We've got a busy day ahead of us; you said so yourself."

"Smooth guy, eh? Has anyone ever told you that you're a brat, Mya?"

She gawked at him. "I am not!"

Laughing, he retorted, "Yeah, that's exactly what a brat would say."

Her eyes flared with mock rage, but she couldn't keep her mouth from tilting up into a smile.

"Get over here and let me wash your hair."

Complying to his demand, because it was a demand and not a request, she closed the distance between them, turning her back and tilting her head under the water. Cascading down her body, the water calmed her overactive brain, and when Lucas started to run shampoo through the strands, she almost melted under his touch.

Massaging her scalp with strong fingers, Mya was aware of his dick as it continued to graze her backside each time he twisted or turned to get to another part of her head. Surprised he wasn't making a move on her as he did something so intimate as washing her hair, she was even more surprised when he spoke to her, emotion and understanding in his words. "I know today might not be the easiest for you, so if you need something from me to help make it better, I need you to tell me."

As he rinsed the suds from her hair, she spoke, eyes closed to shield them from the soap. "I think I'm actually okay." Finding it easier to talk if she wasn't looking at him, she continued as he applied conditioner, relishing in the feeling of human contact. "I know I've only had a few days to process things, but if I'm being completely honest with myself, which I'm usually not that good at, I think I always knew that I wasn't cut out for the big happily ever after. Or at least, that I wasn't going to find it with Dave."

"Why don't you think that you are cut out for happily ever after?"

She mulled over the answer in her mind, trying to come up with the best way to word it, but came up empty. "It's just not who I am." Mya knew it was a cop-out answer, but she wasn't ready to be completely vulnerable with Lucas, needing to keep some of her walls in place.

Thankful that Lucas didn't push the issue, they finished their shower in relative silence, and while Lucas wanted to do nothing but run his hands over her slippery body, he resisted the temptation for both their sakes.

After being cleansed of their night of post-coital bliss, Lucas found the smallest pair of sweats he could find, tossing them to Mya. The clothes dwarfed her slim frame, and she laughed as she rolled the top band of the pants down several times, praying to God that they didn't cascade to the floor when she took a few tentative steps.

Lucas eyed her with hawk-like precision, watching as she gently finger-combed her hair. He had quickly found that when it came to Mya, he was perfectly content to watch her perform the most mundane tasks, and he looked at her with awe while she did.

Coming up behind her, he wrapped his arms around her torso, catching her eye in the mirror she stood in front of. He simply could not keep his hands off of her. Nuzzling her neck, he grinned into her skin when she dropped her head to the side, giving him easier access to gently nip at her freshly washed skin. "I thought you looked sexy in that little black dress last night but seeing you in my clothes might just be the sexiest fucking thing I've ever seen in my life."

Turning to face Lucas while still encircled in his arms, she placed a gentle kiss on his lips. "Half the time, I think you are a wolf in sheep's clothing. Then, you say things like that, and I get a feeling you're actually a bit of a romantic."

"Oh, baby girl," he all but purred in response, "You want romance, I'll give you romance. But first, we need to get down to the shop before I slide those sweats off of you and keep you in my bed. All. Fucking. Day."

Without waiting for a response, he took her hand in his and led Mya towards her first day at Winston's Flowers.

Chapter Fourteen

Feeling wholly out of her element, Mya paced around the workroom of the flower shop while Lucas busied himself collecting buds and blooms from several large, glass-front refrigerators. Being used to knowing exactly what needed to be done and in what timeframe she had to complete her tasks, she felt the anxiety rising from deep within her stomach.

The store was quiet this early in the morning, not opening for several hours. A mixture of floral notes as well as brewing coffee filled the space while the only noise came from Lucas milling about. The back door to the store, probably where deliveries were received, Mya thought, was propped open, and the early morning summer air sent a gentle breeze into the room.

Lucas placed the flowers on the oversized worktable before quickly grabbing several vases, twine, and ribbons. "Come-sit here." He directed Mya to a stool before sitting down next to her. His hand reached out to a manilla folder much like the one he presented Mya with at the restaurant just a few days earlier. Flipping open the sturdy folder, he pulled a picture from it and set it down in front of Mya.

She studied the picture, noticing that many of the blooms scattered about the table looked to be similar to what was in the photo in both size and color. Mya's eyes darted between the picture and fresh flowers several times as she tried to wrap her brain around how all the pieces worked together to create a finished, beautiful arrangement. She was confident in her job as an interior designer. She had worked hard over the years and knew how to turn a blank space into something personal, inviting, and beautiful. But this…this was completely out of her element. "I honestly have no idea how you do it," she said.

"Well today, you're going to learn," he replied.

When Mya originally agreed to this arrangement with Lucas, she knew she would be spending time alongside him, that she would be helping him with deliveries before the gala and that she would be expected to do simple things like help with set-up on the night of the event. But she never expected she would actually be *making* something from the beautiful blossoms and buds. This had to be some type of cruel punishment he was inflicting upon her for her initial reluctance to agree to his terms. Certainly, she thought, there was no way she would be able to make anything that remotely resembled the beautiful pieces of art that Lucas molded with his hands.

She looked at the man sitting next to her as he watched her expectantly. When she made no haste to move, he leaned towards her, pulling the stool she sat on closer to himself. Mya was so close to Lucas that their knees knocked. Bending into her, he placed a tender kiss on her lips. "You're nervous."

Mya was nervous, nervous about making a monstrosity out of what Lucas was asking her to do, but she was also suddenly unnerved by just how well Lucas could read her. In fact, it seemed like since their very first meeting at Winston's, he had been able to see through her sky-high walls.

"What do you want, Ms. Monroe?" Those words echoed through her head now, remembering when he first spoke them last fall.

Even now, she didn't know what she wanted. Did she want Lucas? Her body sure as hell did, even if her mind was at odds with the idea. The struggle between the two feelings swirled in her head, dizzying her. The back room of Winston's Flowers seemed to shrink around her. Mya's senses were on high alert, being attacked by everything from the silence in the room, to the smells swirling in the space. She needed out of the shop.

Pushing back on the stool, she stood and paced back and forth across the concrete floor several times, the slightly too large flip-flops slapping against her heels.

"Mya," Lucas's voice was stern, "talk to me, Sunflower."

But she couldn't talk, couldn't even look at him. Eyes darting around the room, she settled on the small clutch she had taken with her the night before.

"Mya." While he was standing just several steps away, his voice sounded like an echo bouncing off deep cavern walls.

Her gaze snapped to his, rivulets of sweat beading on her forehead. She looked pained, distant.

Mya took one last look between her clutch and Lucas, taking a last look at the beautiful man in front of her.

The beautiful man who played her body like an instrument, the beautiful man who worshiped her body and challenged her mind, the beautiful man who wanted to claim her.

And in that instant, she knew she wasn't ready to be claimed by anyone.-even Lucas Gentry.

Squeezing her eyes tightly shut, she opened them, keeping her gaze averted from his. Quietly, so quietly it was barely a whisper, she spoke, "I'm sorry, Lucas."

And with those three simple words, she grabbed her clutch from the counter and jetted to the back door.

Mya didn't stop when she heard Lucas calling after her, his voice laced with an indecipherable emotion. She didn't stop when she passed April who greeted her with a warm welcome on her way in through the back door. She didn't stop for the traffic or the cyclists careening towards Central Park for their morning ride.

Only once she walked into her penthouse was she able to stop her feet from moving of their own accord, and though her feet had stopped, her mind continued to reel as she spiraled between what she wanted for herself and what she knew was expected of her from almost everyone she knew.

Not knowing why, Mya chose to stay in the over-sized sweats she had borrowed from Lucas, despite the warm summer weather. Inhaling deeply, she let the crisp and unique scent of him assault her senses. Collapsing on the couch, clutch thrown on the coffee table in front of her, she felt like crying though no tears would flow.

Her phone buzzed in her clutch, as it had done repeatedly on her brisk walk home. Knowing it would be Lucas, she wanted to ignore it. But on the off chance it might have been something related to the wedding that was supposed to be happening that morning, she took her chance and pulled it from the bag.

Lucas: **Talk to me, Mya.**

Lucas: **Come back and tell me what the hell is going on.**

Lucas: **Jesus Christ, Mya, at least tell me you're somewhere safe.**

As she stared at the phone, talking herself out of responding to Lucas's text messages, another came though, the buzz from the phone in her hand breaking the spell she was under. Surprised at the name that flashed over her screen, she hesitantly tapped over to the message.

Dave: **Today was supposed to be our day. Instead I'm sitting here alone wondering where we went wrong. Mya, I miss you desperately. Can I please come home so we can work through this together?**

A self-deprecating laugh filled the room as she read and re-read the message before tossing the phone to the other end of the sectional as if it were a bomb poised to explode. There were a lot of things Mya was unsure of. Reconciliation with Dave was not one of them.

She fell into a restless sleep on her couch, waking a few hours later to the sound of the buzzer announcing a guest as it rang through the silent apartment. Lucas or Dave? Her mind bounced between the two men as she walked to the wall that held the intercom before tentatively pushing the button to connect to the doorman below.

"Yes?"

A voice boomed over the intercom, slightly distorted by static coursing through the airways. "Ms. Monroe, there is a Ms. Leary here to see you."

Relief washed over her body, and she pressed the button. "Thank you. Please send her up."

Less than two minutes later, the elevator to the apartment slid open, and Charlotte bounded out, walking towards Mya with a bag of takeout firmly grasped in hand. She hugged Mya without putting the bag down, and though Mya was not usually an affectionate person, she fell into her friend's hug, wrapping her arms tightly around Charlotte's small frame.

Breaking apart, her friend studied her for a beat, lips pursed tightly together. "Those are *definitely* not your clothes."

The two women walked further into the penthouse, Mya stopping to grab her phone from the couch before each grabbing a seat at the island. Mya's mind flashed to the last time she sat at this spot, the night Lucas had pushed her to the precipice of need and want before taking her over the edge. Pushing the thought from her mind, she glanced at her phone.

Lucas: **We had an agreement, Mya.**

Lucas: **I'm not finished with you yet, Sunflower.**

Lucas: **The woman you were with last night came by to look for you.**

Lucas: **Remember, Mya, I always get what I want.**

Unpacking the bag as the aroma of Thai food filled the space, Charlotte looked to her friend, studying Mya's features. "Is this about what today was supposed to be or about something that happened last night?"

"Yes," was Mya's only response to her friend.

Taking the lid off a container of food, Charlotte deeply inhaled the steam pouring off the food. "Come on, Mya. Tell momma Char-Char what happened?"

Mya laughed, the first genuine laugh she had all day. Although her friend was two years younger than herself, Charlotte had a mothering quality and knew when to cut to the chase, leaving her normal silly jokes and prodding aside.

As the women sat and ate, Mya confided in her friend, telling her about the conflicted feelings she had for Lucas. She told her how she felt compelled to escape from the flower shop this morning, about how she couldn't quite figure out if he wanted her as a partner in life or simply as someone to warm their bedsheets with.

"He just…" Mya sighed, not wanting to talk about her experience with Lucas out loud but needing guidance. "He's different. Dark."

Feeling extremely uncomfortable with her lack of experience in the bedroom, she averted her gaze, pushing a piece of chicken around on the plate in front of her.

Ever intuitive, Charlotte pushed slightly, determined to help her friend work through her emotions. "Different and dark doesn't always mean bad, babe. Do you think he would physically hurt you? And not in the bend you over and smack your ass way, but the real, intentional way."

Again, Mya's mind flashed back to their first night together. Lucas's strong palm raining down over her tender ass, his hands tightly woven through her tresses as he pounded into her mouth relentlessly. Parts of that night had hurt, but she didn't know if the physical pain or emotional pain of being humiliated by the man was worse. Still, somewhere deep within her belly, the memories of that night ignited the now-familiar flame of lust and she found herself pressing her thighs together, desperate for his skilled touch.

Deciding the only way to really work through her internal conflict was to use her voice, which was so often silenced throughout her life. "I don't think he would ever hurt me in a traditional sense. Certainly, I don't think he is violent. He's just not…" Mya trailed off, unaware of how to finish the sentence.

Charlotte seemed to sense the way the conversation was going, supplying the answer Mya was unable to speak herself. "Not Dave?"

Nodding her head, Mya tried to put words to her feelings. "He texted today, asked if he could come home so we could work through things together. Dave has just always been what I've known. He's…safe."

Looking at her friend with a cautious gaze, Charlotte replied. "Is it that he is safe, or is it that he is the safe choice for what you *think* is expected of you? Seriously, Mya, is it safe to always wonder if he's cheating on you? Is it safe to walk around on eggshells making sure your heart doesn't continually end up broken?"

Mya tried to speak, but her friend continued on, "I know Lucas Gentry isn't exactly the type of man the Monroe's had in mind for their little girl, and I'm not even saying that it has to be Lucas. But Mya, I saw the way he looked at you at the bar. That man only has eyes for you."

The conversation was interrupted by the buzzer sounding through the apartment again. Sensing Mya's hesitance to answer, Charlotte padded to the entryway, pressing the intercom. "Mya Monroe's residence, how can I help you?"

Mya gently laughed from the kitchen, silently thanking her friend for handling her personal issues just as much as she did her professional issues.

"Afternoon, ma'am. I have a delivery for Ms. Monroe. May I send it up?" The static voice filled the entryway as Mya scanned her brain for any delivery she was expecting, coming up empty.

Charlotte quipped back into the box. "Sure thing. Send it up!"

Waiting by the elevator door, Charlotte was the first to see the oversized display the in-building concierge delivered, and when she loudly cursed, Mya turned, eyes growing wide.

"What the fuck, Mya?" Her friend was almost doubled over in laughter as she took the arrangement, bringing it to the kitchen island.

Mya quickly reached out to the small card placed between varying deep red and burgundy blooms. Hesitating for only an instant, she opened the envelope, recognizing Lucas's handwriting.

Sunflower,

I've only had a small taste of you.

I want so much more.

Yours,

Lucas

Passing the card to Charlotte, who was almost bouncing with excited anticipation, she reiterated her friend's words. "What the fuck indeed."

Chapter Fifteen

After Charlotte left the penthouse, Mya wasn't sure that she was any closer to knowing what she was going to do about Lucas, but she knew that Dave was certainly not the answer. She didn't text Dave back, deciding instead to delete the message, not wanting to see his name each time she opened her messaging app.

She read back through the messages Lucas had sent her, and after not giving herself time to back out, she sent a quick message.

Mya: **The flowers were beautiful. I ask that you please give me some space.**

His response was instantaneous, and Mya became nervous as she watched three dots dance across the bottom of her phone screen.

Lucas: **Anything you need, Sunflower. I'll have your dress and shoes couriered to your building.**

Mya: **Thank you. I will do the same with your clothing as soon as I have them laundered.**

Lucas: **They're yours to keep, baby. Besides, they look better on you anyway.**

Even though he was several blocks away, she still flushed under his generous praise.

Playing back her earlier conversation with Charlotte, she couldn't help but think that her friend had a point. Mya had seen how protective Lucas was over her. She saw how attentive he was to her needs, always making sure she was cared for and feeling okay with what they did in the bedroom. He made her feel sexy, sexier than she had ever felt before in her life.

Taking one last look at the flowers he had sent, she walked over to the pile of paint supplies that were still scattered on the floor and set about making a place where she could pursue her passion.

While it took nearly an hour, Mya was able to look at the space she carved out for her painting area with pride. She still needed a few more shelves to hold all the painting accessories, but for now, her makeshift studio would do.

With acanvas perched upon the easel, Mya moved

to place several blobs of paint onto a fresh palette. Growing up, before she stopped painting, she always preferred having a palette that was well loved, showing stains of projects past.

Before choosing a few brushes to work with, she placed a record on, letting the sounds of mournful classical music fill the space. Mya didn't feel particularly mournful, but the music seemed to power her creative process.

Hands moving of their own accord, they quickly bathed the canvas in smooth strokes of gentle pinks and beiges. Large flowers, like the ones Lucas had pulled from the refrigerators that morning, filled the canvas. She didn't know the names of the blooms, but it didn't stop them from being any less alluring. Sage green leaves of various sizes filled in the white space, spilling over to the edges of the wrapped canvas. Mya ran small white highlights on the tips of some petals and leaves, showing where natural sun would hit them in the wild. Thankful for the long dry time of oil paints, she took her time in making sure her first painting in years was as close to perfection as she could get.

Stepping back and staring at her work, a sense of pride coursed through her body. Mya wanted to share her creation with someone, wanted someone else to feel proud of her the way she currently felt about herself. Sure, she could show Charlotte and knew her friend would be ecstatic that Mya was finally doing something for herself. But really, the only person she wanted to show was Lucas.

She wouldn't, though.

She couldn't.

She couldn't put herself back in his path and fall for the man deeper than she already had until she was absolutely sure it was the right decision. And that was a decision she wasn't ready to make.

Instead, she took one last look at the painting before cleaning her supplies, pouring herself a glass of wine, and crawling into her bed, still in Lucas's clothing and despite the fact that the sun had not yet set.

Thankful that she had limited her wine intake the day before, Mya woke Sunday morning without a hangover. Still, she didn't feel rested after a full night comprised mostly of tossing and turning.

She tried every trick in the book to get a few uninterrupted hours-meditation, quiet music, counting sheep, melatonin, diffusing some essential oils-but nothing seemed to help.

Taking in her room, the room she once considered her sanctuary, it now felt hollow. Empty.

Briefly, she considered getting a pet, thinking it would help to add warmth to her life, but she couldn't help but think she'd just mess up an animal's life the way she felt she had messed up her own.

Peeling herself from her bed, she walked to the door, quickly glancing at the still blooming sunflowers spilling from her favorite vase before walking towards her living space in search of her phone.

Mya glanced at her phone, seeing her mother had texted her three times to remind her of their scheduled brunch that afternoon. It was just after 8:00 A.M. and Mya silently cursed the person who taught her mother how to text as the phone buzzed in her hand, signaling yet another onslaught of messages from her mother.

Mom: **Mya, dear, I really wish you would answer me.**

Mom: **I understand you are upset about David, but you simply must move on from here.**

Lord help Mya, she thought while rolling her eyes despite the fact that no one could see her. This was going to be a long day.

It had always bothered Mya that her mother

insisted on calling Dave by his full name. Diane Monroe was the only person who referred to him as David. His own parents didn't even call him by his full name, calling him Dave or more frequently by his childhood nickname of DD.

More than being bothered by her mother's use of Dave's full name though, was how confused she was. What had her mother meant about moving "on from here." What the hell did that even mean? Was her mother expecting her to move on *with* Dave? Because while she still had a lot of unanswered questions in her own mind, she knew there was a better chance of the city eradicating the population of subway rats before she reconciled with Dave.

Mya sent a quick message to her mother, confirming she would be at brunch. Her stomach took that as the perfect opportunity to remind her that it had been hours since she had eaten, announcing its dissatisfaction with a low growl. As she started towards the kitchen in search of something to tide her over, the apartment buzzer rang.

As Mya walked toward the intercom, she couldn't help but chuckle when she realized the buzzer had rung more in the last week than it had in the previous year.

She pressed the button, and the familiar sound of static echoed into the entryway.

"Ms. Monroe, so sorry to bother you this early," the concierge spoke nervously. "A delivery just arrived for you. Is it okay to send it up, or would you like me to hold onto it until later?"

Mya smiled at the apprehensiveness of the concierge, assuring him no apology was necessary before giving him permission to bring up the delivery.

After her brief text exchange with Lucas, she expected the delivery to simply be the dress and shoes she had left at his apartment after her abrupt departure.

As the elevator doors slid open, Mya gasped, another gigantic flower arrangement meeting her, so large, she could barely make out the young man who brought the arrangement to her penthouse. Juggling the arrangement as well as a small bag, Mya profusely thanked the concierge before making her way to the kitchen, placing this arrangement next to the one that was delivered the day before.

Unlike the previous arrangement which was made from many different blooms, this one was made of almost entirely the same flower in varying sizes and hues. Muted beiges, dusty pinks, and pure white gerbera daisies were held by sturdy stems in a nearly opaque vase with just a hint of eucalyptus tucked throughout. Simple yet elegant, Mya imagined the vase sitting on a blanket in a meadow, a delicious picnic splayed on the blanket as spring warmth grazed her skin.

Peeking into the bag that accompanied the flower delivery, she found her dress and shoes as expected. On top of the neatly folded garment, an envelope sat with Mya's name written in script. Lifting it from the small bag, she held it in her hand for a moment as if weighing the implications that opening it would have on her life. Of course, the temptation won over, and she opened the envelope, pulling out a small card embossed with pastel flowers on the front.

Sunflower,

Beauty, innocence, and purity.

I think of all three when I see the gerbera daisy.

But I also think of you.

Yours,

Lucas

Mya's heart stuttered in her chest, beating irregularly as she lightly traced the words with her fingers. It made her long for the man, long for the way he made her feel both emotionally and physically.

She wanted to run to Lucas in that moment, throw her arms around his neck, kiss his full lips, and run her hands over the now familiar landscape of his chest. Mya wanted Lucas Gentry; she knew it in her heart that she did.

But she couldn't do it.

She wouldn't do it until she was absolutely sure that her brain matched what her heart wanted. Until the two were no longer at war with one another, she would keep her distance from Lucas, silently praying that when the time came, he would still want her just as badly as she was beginning to want him.

And while she wanted to work out the conflict between her two organs at that very moment, wanted to be able to run to Lucas, tell him that he was right and that they did belong together, she first had to prepare for brunch with Diane Monroe.

Chapter Sixteen

Tavern On The Green was a New York City staple. Originally built as a sheepfold for over 700 sheep that once grazed Central Park, it had long since been transformed into a premier dining location. Actors, musicians, political figures, and New York City elite flocked to the restaurant through the late 1970s and it was still a sought-after location for gourmet meals and sweeping views of Central Park.

Of course, Mya thought as she strode through the double doors with purpose, it was exactly the type of place her mother would choose for brunch.

After giving her mother's name to the hostess, Mya was ushered to the opulent Crystal Room. Oversized chandeliers hung from the ornately decorated ceiling.

Huge floral arrangements flanked the room, and they immediately made Mya think of Lucas.

Expecting brunch to be just her and her parents, she was surprised to find her mother and father sitting at a large table with several empty seats to either side.

Both parents stood, her impeccably dressed mother air-kissing her on each cheek while her father, forever cold, opted for a quick hug.

The trio sat, Mya looking to her parents expectantly.

Her mother was the first to speak, an exaggerated breathy cadence that gave off an air of superiority. "The rest of our party will be along shortly, dear. Would you care for a mimosa while we wait?"

"Who else is joining us?" A pit formed in Mya's stomach. Whatever her mother and father were planning, it surely was not good.

Ignoring her question, Diane flagged down a nearby server, ordering a mimosa on her daughter's behalf.

Mark, her father, looked at his wife, shaking his head in a disapproving manner. Her parents had been married for over thirty years, and Mya could count on her hands how many times she had seen them show genuine affection to each other. While she never had proof, she believed both had affairs outside their marriage, choosing to stay with one another for the social standing and financial cushion it provided.

Two drinks later, Mya was starting to feel a nice buzz as her family continued to wait for the rest of their party to arrive. Her parents mostly talked to her, not with her. And while Mya did her best to nod at appropriate times and throw semi-interested interjections into the conversation, she mostly let them speak while wishing she was at Lucas's apartment, wrapped in his arms and covered in his oversized sweats.

Lifting her glass flute to her lips, Mya stopped, dumbfounded as Dave and his parents made their way through the Crystal Room to their table. Her cheeks heated with anger, and she found herself downing the rest of the cool liquid in the glass, glaring at the man who had crushed her with absolute daggers in her eyes.

Diane and Mark stood, repeating the same greeting they had with Mya just a short time earlier. Mya didn't move, frozen in place with a mixture of ire and confusion. As Dave's parents, Irene and Martin, took their seats, Dave came to Mya's side, pressing an unwanted chaste kiss to her cheek while his hand rested on her shoulder.

"I've missed you so much, Mya." He spoke low, making sure only he and Mya could hear his words.

Her body tensed under his touch, but if Dave

noticed, he didn't do anything about it, simply taking the seat next to her.

The server came, taking the drink order of the Donaldson family, and while they spoke to the young woman in charge of their table, Mya did everything in her power to think of a reason to push her chair back from the table, any excuse to make her escape from what had quickly become her own personal hell.

She could do this, she thought to herself. She could get through this one, simple brunch, and hopefully by the end of the meal, her family would agree that she and Dave would not be reconciling.

As the server returned with their drinks, Diane lifted her own glass, offering a toast to the table. "It's so lovely of you all to join us today. I know this weekend did not go as planned, but I am thankful that we have all been able to come together today to put the past behind us."

Mya tried to speak. "Mom…"

Mark cut his daughter off. "Don't interrupt your mother, Mya. You know that is quite rude."

Mya sat, mouth agape. It was rude of her to interrupt her mother, but it wasn't rude of her father to interrupt her while she was interrupting her mother?

As her mother finished speaking, everyone at the table, Dave included, lifted their glasses, clinking with one another-everyone except Mya.

Dave placed his hand on Mya's thigh under the table. She quickly shifted in her chair, enough to make his hand fall away from her body.

The men broke off into chatter about business dealings as the woman talked about upcoming events, Mya refusing more than a simple yes or no answer when asked a direct question. She was still trying to come up with some way out of this abhorrent brunch when Irene mentioned the upcoming Night of a Million Stars gala-the very gala she was supposed to be working alongside Lucas to execute. As if a proverbial lightbulb turned on above her head, she quickly formed a plan, hoping it would work.

Excusing herself to the bathroom, she escaped to the silence of a bathroom stall, sliding her phone from the purse she brought with her. Not giving herself time to second guess herself, she sent a text to the only person who could save her from this situation.

***Mya:* I desperately need your help.**

Lucas's response was instant.

***Lucas:* Anything for you, Sunflower.**

***Mya:* How fast can you get to Tavern On The Green?**

***Lucas:* I just finished setting up a ceremony at Summit Rock. Probably about 20?**

Mya's mind reeled. Summit Rock was *in* Central

Park. Lucas was basically already here. This could actually freaking work!

Her fingers flew over the keyboard in response.

Mya: **Came to meet my parents for brunch. They blindsided me by having Dave and his parents show.**

Lucas: **I'm already on my way, Mya.**

For the first time since sitting down with her parents, a genuine smile threatened to break out across her face. God, what did she do to deserve this man?

Mya rejoined her party at the table, thankful for once that her family enjoyed drawing out their overly fancy meals. They had ordered appetizers, but wanting a leisurely brunch, still had not ordered their main course. Hopefully, this would give Lucas enough time to reach her.

Roasted figs and smoked salmon were being passed around the table, and as Mya plated a fig, drizzling it with a bit of extra honey, shivers ran over her body. Automatically, she knew Lucas had entered the space, and when she lifted her eyes from her plate, she was rewarded with the beautiful bearded man stalking toward their table.

Lucas was dressed in slim, navy dress pants and a subtle pinstripe dress shirt. Sleeves rolled up, his delicious, muscular forearms were on display. Tan shoes and matching colored belt completed the look and along with his now neatly trimmed beard and styled hair, he looked every part the stylish afternoon brunch goer. Mya couldn't decide if she liked this look or his casual everyday look better.

His dangerous blue eyes locked with hers, a small nod of his chin almost signaling to Mya as if to say, "I've got this."

He reached the table, and Mya stood to greet him. Without warning, he pulled her close, wrapping her in a hug as mouths all around the table hung open. Lucas kissed Mya, but unlike the chaste kiss on her cheek from Dave, he had tilted her chin towards him and captured her lips with his.

Releasing her lips, he turned towards her parents, correctly assuming which couple at the table were related to her based on their close resemblance. "Mr. and Mrs. Monroe, a pleasure to meet you. Sorry for running late; I was just finishing up an event in the park. Your lovely daughter didn't tell me we'd have an audience for our introduction today," he motioned towards the rest of the table with one hand, his other firmly clasped around Mya's.

One by one, each person stood, Lucas shaking hands with each. Seizing the opportunity before him, Lucas sat in the seat Dave had previously been sitting in, shooting Mya a quick wink that had her clenching her thighs under the table as she retook her seat.

He had come.

Not only had he come, but he was playing the *hell* out of the situation.

Diane broke the awkward silence stretching around the table. "I'm so very sorry, young man. I do not believe I caught your name?" Mya's mom may have been the type of woman who preferred getting manicures to managing a business, but nonetheless, she was smart.

Speaking before Lucas could, Mya made the introduction. "Mom and Dad, this is Lucas Gentry."

Dave coughed, liquid from his mouth sputtering down his chin. His voice was loud when he spoke, causing several other tables to momentarily turn their gaze towards them. "The FLORIST?" He said it with such incredulity that Mya almost laughed. "Mya, baby, I understand being upset with me over what happened, but is it really necessary for you to act out like this and seek revenge with another man, let alone with a vendor from *our* wedding?"

All eyes turned to her, and she felt heat creeping up her cheeks. Bracing herself to speak, she felt a strong reassuring squeeze on her thigh before Lucas took control of the conversation once again. "Dave, is it?" Lucas knew it was, in fact, Dave, but he wasn't going to let Dave know that. "I guess I really do have you to thank for this."

He stretched out one arm, resting it casually on Mya's seat back before returning his attention to Dave. "If it wasn't for your wandering eyes…and hands… and well…other parts…" Lucas trailed off, not finishing the sentence.

Dave's face flared while his knuckles turned white as he grasped the edge of the table forcefully. One corner of Lucas's mouth ticked up in a smile as he accepted the bottle of beer the server placed in front of him. Offering a glass, Lucas declined the server's gesture, instead lifting the bottle to his lips. He took a long pull before setting the bottle back on the table.

Four sets of eyes stared at the unlikely trio of Mya, Lucas, and Dave. While the silence stretched, Lucas gently cut the fig still sitting on Mya's plate before offering her a bite off her fork. They may have been sitting with Mya's parents, her ex-fiancé, and his family, but Lucas couldn't help but watch intently as her perfect, red lips parted, making way for him to slide the fork between them. Just the simple thought of those lips wrapped around his dick once again made him hard.

Irene's voice broke Lucas's thoughts. "Will someone please tell me what on Earth is happening?"

Having Lucas next to her, Mya had a sudden burst of bravery. "Well, after I found Dave sleeping with my maid of honor, I took it upon myself to take the helm on canceling all the wedding plans. Lucas and I met to talk about donating flowers that had already arrived for the wedding, and over the course of a few days of planning, we really hit it off." She left out the part about how the man had given her several of the most intense orgasms of her life, deciding that was information that didn't need to be shared.

Several gasps could be heard, echoing around the table

Martin fixed his gaze on his son's face, "You said Mya had gotten cold feet?"

Dave was actually squirming in his seat, his face not any less red than it had been several minutes earlier.

All eyes turned to Dave.

Lucas, smirking from across the table, simply enjoyed the other man's impending breakdown while knowing the humiliation he was feeling today was nothing in comparison to what he had put Mya through.

Diane and Mark looked to their daughter as if waiting for her to fill in more of the blanks. After a long sigh, Mya spoke softly, the words directed toward everyone at the table. Her eyes met each one of them as she spoke. "There is no chance of reconciliation. I simply cannot allow myself to be treated as second best, and if this entire situation has taught me anything, it is that I deserve to be someone's priority."

Pushing her chair back, she stood, looking at her stunned parents.

Mya next looked at Lucas, fire in her eyes. "Would you like to go get food from somewhere else? It seems like the rest of the table has some catching up to do." Turning towards her parents, she continued, "I'll give you a call this week, and we can talk more. Right now, I just need some time."

Lucas stood as she finished speaking, placing his hand on her lower back. "I'd like nothing more, Sunflower." Looking at Mya's parents, he tipped his head. "It was a pleasure to meet you both. Hopefully, next time it will be under better circumstances."

Chapter Seventeen

Sitting across from one another at a diner halfway between both of their apartments, Lucas and Mya found themselves laughing easily as they stuffed their faces with greasy burgers and fries. Mya was surprised at how easily the conversation had flowed through their meal. It somehow felt different than their interactions in the past. It felt…nice.

"I know I've already said it at least fifty times, but I'm going to say it at least once more. I cannot thank you enough for today. Truly."

Lucas slid his hand across the table, covering Mya's delicate hand with his larger, calloused fingers. "And every time you do thank me, I'm going to tell you that it was no problem." He gave her hand a little squeeze.

"And honestly, I like that you thought of me when you needed something, even if it was just an act."

Mya winced at his words, realizing that she had been the equivalent of emotional whiplash to the poor man sitting across from her. Lucas had been nothing but forthcoming with her, and she owed him truth in reciprocity.

Earnestness danced across her face as she looked down at their hands. Mya pulled her hand from under the heaviness of his touch, but she didn't retreat. Instead, she linked her fingers through his while nervously averting her eyes. Her voice was quiet, barely a whisper. "It wasn't an act."

Lucas was confident his heart momentarily stopped beating as Mya continued talking, words spilling from her lips like a dam had broken. "I'm scared, Lucas, so damn scared. You're all I've thought about since I left you at the shop. And then, the beautiful flowers and words. And the sex. *God, the sex.*"

Her cheeks heated in embarrassment as she said those last words, and she knew she was babbling, but she simply couldn't stop. "You make me feel beautiful and brave. I mean, I *actually* stood up to my parents today. Twenty-freaking-seven years old and I have never stood up for myself. Until you."

Releasing their entwined fingers only long enough to stand, Lucas slid into the booth next to Mya.

Suddenly overtaken by his larger-than-life presence, she scooted over, trying to make room. Lucas didn't allow her to move away. Instead, he pulled her into his side, wrapping one strong arm around her back, letting it drape over her shoulders.

With his other hand, he reached forward, grabbing a fry from Mya's plate on the table, popping it into his mouth.

Mya watched as he chewed several times before swallowing, his Adam's apple bobbing up and down, his jaw strong. Carefully considering what he wanted to say, he used the fries as an opportunity to gather his thoughts.

"You have a tendency to steal food from other people, don't you?"

He took one last fry, shooting Mya a sly wink as he swallowed. "So, here's the thing, babe. You *are* beautiful and brave. You deserve flowers and words every damn day. And sex, too."

A grin spread across his face, a naughty glint in his eyes. Using the arm that was still across Mya's shoulders, he pulled her even closer, dropping a kiss against the top of her head. Lucas didn't hold her in place, but at the same time, she made no attempt to move from the comfortable spot under his arm.

They sat in silence for several minutes, both

enjoying the company the other provided-not talking. Simply existing.

Mya sighed against Lucas, the bravery he seemed to instill in her slowly building. "I want to rewrite the arrangement."

Lucas slowly pushed away, not wanting to lose her warmth but needing to see her face, to look at her eyes. "Tell me what you want, and I'll make it happen."

The waitress stopped by their table, clearing a few dishes and dropping off a small leather folder which contained their check. Mya moved to grab it from the end of the table, but Lucas was faster.

"Please, it's the least I can do after what you did for me today."

Lucas tucked a few bills into the folder, sliding it to the edge of the table. "I didn't do anything for you today that I didn't want to."

Standing, he offered his hand to Mya. She graciously accepted, and he tugged her to her feet. "Too full for dessert?"

Mya had an undeniable sweet tooth. While she tried her hardest to keep it under control, she almost always craved something with thick, sugary frosting. It's exactly why she was so dedicated to her spin classes. She hated exercise-abhorred it. But she was a woman torn between looking like a snack and wanting to eat every sweet snack in sight, so it was a necessary evil in her life. Shaking her head, she smiled. "Never."

"Happy Endings? We can grab something and talk more about what you'd like to change about our arrangement."

Her smile widened, though she wasn't sure if it was because Lucas was willing to discuss their arrangement or because he brought up the name of her favorite local New York City dessert bar.

The pair grabbed a cab and headed towards Tribeca. As the driver weaved in and out of New York City traffic, only almost hitting one bike courier, the easy conversation continued between the two. Neither was sure when it happened, but when the cab arrived outside the dessert bar, they found they were holding hands, fingers entwined. Lucas reluctantly released her hand, preparing to pay for their cab fare. But before he could wrangle his wallet from his back pocket, Mya pulled out her debit card, almost as if from thin air, and swiped it through the meter in the backseat. She giggled at Lucas as he sat there, silently stunned, before she leaned over and gave him a quick kiss on the cheek. Pushing open the door of the cab, she called after, "Going to have to be quicker than that next time, big guy!"

Lucas laughed, running a hand through his thick beard before thanking the driver and exiting the cab.

He couldn't figure out exactly when Mya had started to let her guard down with him, he just knew that he would do anything to keep it that way-to keep her laughing, to keep her smiling.

For the second time that afternoon, Mya and Lucas found themselves together in a small booth. Only this time, Lucas chose to sit on the same side of the booth as Mya the entire time. She shot him a glance, narrowing her hazel eyes at him.

"What? It's easier to share this way."

She laughed, playfully bumping his shoulder with hers. "Oh, no. Who said anything about sharing? You do *not* want to get between me and my sweets!"

Mya was still trying to decide what she wanted when their server approached. "Ugh! I just can't make up my mind! This happens every flipping time!"

Lucas laughed at Mya. He always thought she was sexy, but when she inserted words like "flipping" instead of "fucking," it was downright cute. "Tell you what," he spoke to the server, "bring us one of everything on the menu and a bottle of your best champagne."

He plucked the menu from a stunned Mya's fingers and handed both his and hers to the server who just stared at him with wide eyes.

Happy Endings was a kitschy little spot. Pink vinyl booths lined the walls while equally bright purple damask wallpaper coved the place from floor to ceiling. Oversized framed pictures featured the multitude of celebrities that had been to the location, posing with desserts, and big, glittery chandeliers hung throughout from the ceiling. The restaurant was known for only serving high-end desserts, milkshakes, and top-shelf drinks and was a popular place for locals, tourists, and bachelorette parties alike.

Their server flitted away when she realized Lucas was serious, her high ponytail swishing from side to side, pert ass swaying as she retreated to the kitchen. Lucas couldn't help but think that this woman would have been exactly his type at some point, the type of woman who immediately turned him on. The type of woman he quickly took to bed. But now, looking at the woman as she sashayed away with wide hips swaying, he felt absolutely nothing. And of course, he knew that was because of the woman sitting next to him.

"I can't believe you actually ordered one of everything! That is like…my ultimate dream!"

Lucas reached for the paper placemat on the table. Covered with simple games like tic-tac-toe and connect the dots, it was just as much for the adults as it was for anyone who happened into the restaurant with kids. However, he wasn't interested in the games. Flipping it over to the blank back side, he motioned to Mya's purse. "If that's your ultimate dream, you've got some serious problems, babe. You got a pen in there?"

She pulled a pen from its perfect place inside her optimally organized purse, handing it to Lucas. "Hey, I don't take spin three times a week for nothing. It's all for the love of dessert."

Mya saw something flash in his eyes, but she couldn't make out what it was. "What was that look for?"

Lucas disregarded the question as he scrawled across the top of the blank placemat, unable to admit to Mya he was suddenly picturing her tight ass in equally tight spandex while she rode a stationary bike, sweat beading on her skin. Looking at the placemat Lucas had written on, Mya could see it read, "The Arrangement."

"Okay, Sunflower. Let me hear your demands."

She blushed as the server dropped off a bottle of champagne and two flutes, pouring each full of the fizzy liquid. Mya took a sip, moaning as the bubbles lightly danced across her tongue.

Lucas took a drink from his own glass before leaning into Mya's ear, his dick twitching at the simple sound that escaped her mouth. "I'm willing to do whatever it takes to keep you in my life, but if you keep making sounds like that, I will *not* be held responsible for my actions."

She squeaked, an honest to goodness squeak, as her eyes widened. "Yeah…" she trailed off before slightly recovering her composure. "Let's stick to what we came here for."

Mya took the pen from Lucas, pulling the placemat so it was directly in front of her. Numbering the left-hand side of the placemat, she started to fill in each blank with her swirly handwriting:

1. Both parties agree to no less than two (2) dates per week to be planned by Mr. Lucas Gentry. On said dates, both parties will actively participate in meaningful conversation to get to know one another better.

2. Ms. Mya Monroe agrees to attend the Night of a Million Stars gala with Mr. Lucas Gentry but will not be held responsible for assisting with setup or breakdown of the aforementioned event.

3. Ms. Mya Monroe agrees to assist Mr Lucas Gentry with the delivery of flowers one day of each weekend on a day of his choosing.

4. Both parties agree to abstain from sex both with one another as well as with other parties for the duration of the Arrangement.

5. Both parties agree that The Arrangement can be broken by either party at any time and for any reason.

6. Both parties agree that The Arrangement can be ratified at any time only if both parties agree to the changes.

7. The ratified arrangement will begin today and last for a duration of four weeks.

She scanned the words she wrote, making sure she didn't miss anything that was important to her. As she was finalizing the hysterical excuse for a binding contract, their server reappeared, a tray overflowing with every type of dessert known to man. The woman placed cakes, cupcakes, pies, brownies, and even some ice cream dishes in front of them. Lucas took the opportunity to quickly grab the placemat, his eyes quickly reading the changes Mya wanted to make to their arrangement.

"Number four," Lucas tapped at Mya's impressive script as the server continued to empty her tray. "Are we talking no sex at all or strictly none of my dick in your pussy?"

Their server's eyes grew large as she blushed, Mya looked absolutely horrified, and Lucas...well, Lucas just laughed. "Just trying to figure out what I'm in for, Sunflower."

After the waitress dropped the last plate on their table, she practically ran away, all the while Mya continued to struggle to regain her composure. Finally finding her words, she said, "No sex, Lucas. I want to get to know you-the real you."

"Can I still hold your hand?" He reached out and took her hand in his.

"Sure."

"Kiss you?" He leaned in and kissed her gently on the lips.

"Okay."

"Run my hands up and down your body and tease you with my fingers?" He lightly traced his fingers up and down her forearm.

"Maybe."

"Lay you down gently on my bed and lick my way to your wet, slippery center?" He leaned in closer, tracing the shell of her ear with his tongue.

"Lucas." Her tone was stern, but her body betrayed her. He watched as her pupils dilated, and her breaths became labored.

"What if I did this?" Lucas reached across the table, swiping his finger through some pink frosting adorning the top of a cupcake. Slowly, he brought the frosting-covered finger to Mya, lightly smearing the thick, sugary frosting over her lips before dipping the finger into his own mouth. Swirling the rest of the frosting off his finger, he shot Mya a wink.

She sat for a minute, frosting covering her lips before uncharacteristically pulling Lucas to her, smooshing the frosting between their lips. He laughed but quickly the kiss turned hungry. Darting his tongue out from between his lips, he licked hers, cleaning the smeared frosting from her beautiful face. Lucas brought a hand up behind Mya, twisting his fingers in her silky black strands. "Sweetest fucking frosting in the entire world, and you still taste sweeter."

Mya found the pen on the table, hidden among the gratuitous number of desserts. Making a small spot in front of her, she speedily jotted down one more point before passing the placemat back to Lucas.

1. Mr. Lucas Gentry is expected to continue to speak to Ms. Mya Monroe in ways that make her swoon and blush.

Lucas laughed, grabbing the pen from her hand. Hastily, he scrawled his name and date on the bottom of the paper before handing it to Mya along with the pen. She also signed, her neat swirly script contrasting his slanted harsh script almost as much as they contrasted each other in real life. Lucas took her champagne glass, condensation beading along the base, and mock stamped it on the paper. "There, now it's been properly notarized."

Mya threw her head back and laughed. He motioned to her champagne glass, and when she had it in hand, toasted to her, the bravery she had that day to stand up to her parents and to their future as they navigated their arrangement together.

Chapter Eighteen

MUCH OF THE next two weeks flew by as Mya and Lucas spent time truly getting to know one another. Lucas held up his end of the agreement, planning memorable dates for Mya. The pair explored unique eateries, visited museums, and even took a trip to a flower market just outside the city where Lucas regularly purchased stock for Winston's Flowers.

Mya found the flower market fascinating. Row after row of vendors stretched out, offering flowers in every color of the rainbow, in all shapes and sizes. As they walked hand and hand through the market, Lucas pointed out unique flowers and their meanings. He pulled her towards a vendor with Black-Eyed Beauty Anemones-his favorite-and as she ran her fingers delicately over the stark white petals and deep charcoal center he explained that the flowers frequently represented anticipation but that the white anemone also represented sincerity.

"I just never knew there were so many meanings behind flowers. It's all actually *really* beautiful."

Steering her towards another booth, he was looking at her, not the flowers, when he responded, "It really is."

They stole small kisses from one another while they strolled through the market, as they so often had over the previous two weeks. There were many moments, *so* many moments, where Lucas wanted to yell, "fuck the arrangement," throw Mya up against the nearest surface he could find, and tear her clothes off with his teeth. But, as strong as the urge was, he stuck to rule four of the arrangement. He had lost track of how many times he muttered, "stupid fucking number four" under his breath and swore that while his two weeks with Mya had been thoroughly enjoyable, they were also the two most frustrating weeks of his life.

Lucas surprised Mya as they were leaving the market, buying her a simple bouquet of sunflowers and Dahlia wrapped in butcher's paper.

"What's the meaning of this one?" She asked the question while studying a bright Dahlia tucked into the bouquet. It was perhaps the most beautiful flower Mya had ever seen. Yellow in the center, it faded into a sea of stunning peaches and pinks. She couldn't wait to paint this flower, as she had become accustomed to doing with all the flowers Lucas brought her or sent her on an almost daily basis.

Lucas loved that she was asking questions, loved that she was showing genuine interest in what he did for a living. Pride surged through him, and he smiled wide before biting down on his lower lip, his slightly chipped front tooth leaving a small indent in his flesh. "Well, there are over 1,000 species of Dahlia alone. The Aztecs used it as a religious symbol, but more commonly, it represents elegance." He swept a stray strand of her black bob behind her ear with gentle fingers. "It represents involvement, staying calm under pressure in challenging situations. It represents commitment to another person. It represents…love."

"Oh." It was merely a whisper, and she suddenly felt the need to avert her eyes from his, aware of how the air seemed to evaporate from the outdoor market.

WHILE LUCAS WAS BUSY PLANNING AND EXECUTING dates to make Mya swoon, she held up her end of the arrangement, too. One day each weekend, they would meet at Winston's Flowers and load up the shop's old box van full of flowers that would otherwise end up becoming trash. Sometimes, the flowers were left over from events while other times, they were simply flowers that hadn't been purchased and were coming up on their expiration date.

After just the first time, Mya decided that it was her favorite day of the week. She came to find that Lucas loved delivering to local long-term care facilities, spending time talking with the residents as he changed out old flower arrangements that were past their prime. It was such a different side of him-a kind, sweet, philanthropic side-and it did things to her insides.

More than once, her stomach flip-flopped as she watched from the corner of her eye while he interacted with residents and staff. It was as if a hundred butterflies had taken up residence in her belly, all fluttering their wings at once. Mya couldn't remember the last time she had felt that way with Dave. Being honest with herself, she didn't know that she ever had.

She also found that as her relationship with Lucas quickly progressed, she spent less and less time thinking about Dave. In fact, Mya could now go several days without ever thinking of the man who was almost her forever. And that felt wonderful.

On their third weekend, Mya entered the flower

shop through the front door, expecting to find April on the sales floor. Instead, an older woman she had only met once before greeted her and waved her through to the back room as she flitted around between several customers. Mya had become comfortable in the space, almost feeling like it was an extension of her home.

Before retreating to the back to meet with Lucas, she walked up to a customer who had yet to be helped and worked with the woman to pick out several different types of flowers to include in a bouquet for her best friend. She had picked up some basic knowledge of the industry from Lucas, learning meanings behind flowers, the best seasons for certain blooms, and frequent pairings. She was a far cry from being as well-versed as Lucas, but she was nowhere near as intimidated as she was when she first came to the shop to help Lucas after spending the night in his bed.

Mya could feel Lucas's eyes on her before she saw him, and when she finished with the woman she had been helping, she turned to find him propped against a nearby wall, a giant smile on his face.

She walked to him, and he pulled her into a hug, kissing the crown of her head as he so often did. "You're a natural, Sunflower. Ever think of giving this a full time shot?"

Recently, Mya had been growing increasingly frustrated with her job, and she didn't hide that fact from

Lucas. She had regained her love of painting, was beginning to find even more ways to be creative, and just wasn't finding the same passion she once had for interior design. Mya wanted to use her hands to build and sculpt and mold something from scratch. So much of her life had been spent simply buying ready-made products and placing them on a shelf. It just wasn't the same anymore.

Looking up into Lucas's blue eyes-eyes that were more Caribbean blue than cornflower blue on that particular day-she searched for a sign that he was joking, but he simply looked at her with a face void of jest.

"You're being serious?"

He shrugged his broad shoulders. "Why wouldn't I be?"

"I can't just walk into a shop and get a job without experience, Lucas."

Now he laughed, the sound booming from deep within his chest and spreading out across the sales floor. He didn't answer with words, simply used an arm to make a sweeping gesture around the shop.

"That's…um…that's a lot to unpack. Can we file that discussion away for later?"

Still chuckling, he tucked her under his arm. "Come on, beautiful; we've got a special stop to make today."

Working in tandem, they loaded the van quickly before climbing into the cab of the vehicle. Lucas took the driver's seat and expertly navigated the city streets, pulling up a short time later into a loading zone outside of a tall building. A young woman met them with two rolling carts and helped to unload the flowers before Lucas took the van to a nearby parking garage.

Mya waited for Lucas in the lobby of the long-term care facility. While they had visited several over the last few weeks, stopping at two to three each time they met, this one was much nicer than the others. The lobby had a seating area with coffee available, a small play-room for kids, and all the staff she spied had on matching uniforms.

When Lucas rejoined her, they wheeled the carts towards the reception desk and the woman behind the counter lit up when she saw him. "Oh, Mr. Gentry, a pleasure to see you as always!"

She was almost overly jovial, but Mya could tell that her happy-go-lucky attitude was genuine.

After procuring visitor badges, they took the elevator to the twelfth floor. The doors opened into a large open area, and what Mya assumed to be residents were busy with all sorts of activities. Several older gentlemen played Wii bowling while women worked on a puzzle nearby. She saw a snack station set up where several others had congregated, and yet, more residents were in the middle of a heated game of bingo.

The same woman who had helped them load the carts came over and began to remove arrangements from the cart. Lucas plucked one off the top of the cart nearest him, and sliding his hand in Mya's, led her down a nearby hallway.

They came to stand outside a door and Lucas stopped before entering, turning to Mya. "I haven't been completely honest with you. This place is extra special to me, Mya. And there is someone here I'd like you to meet."

Her heart rate accelerated and she was sure Lucas could feel how her hand instantly became clammy in his. If he did notice, he chose to ignore it. Pulling her through the door, they entered a spacious residential room.

A small seating area sat off to the right of the room, two women sitting in the chairs looking out over New York City. "Let's get this party started!"

Mya was surprised when the younger of the two women turned around, and she came face to face with April from the flower shop. A stunning older woman also stood, coming to give Lucas an enormous hug before taking the flowers from his outstretched hand.

The woman was small, just over five feet. She had gray hair that had been swept up into a fancy French twist, was well dressed in clothes Mya knew were designer, and when she looked at the woman's face, she noted that her eyes were a carbon copy of Lucas's own baby blues.

"And who is this beautiful young lady?" The woman directed the question to Mya, but Lucas interjected.

"Grandma, I'd like you to meet my good friend, Ms. Mya Monroe. Mya, my grandmother Scarlett Gentry."

Mya extended a hand and was surprised when the small woman pulled her into an equally big hug. Her first instinct was to freeze, but she quickly melted into the woman, bringing her arms around her in return.

Growing up, Mya's family was never affectionate with one another. Sometimes, she thought she could count on one hand how many times her family told one another that they loved each other. They handed out hugs and compliments even less often. Being hugged by the woman she just learned was Lucas's grandmother almost had a familiar feel. It felt like being welcomed home after a long absence.

April came over, greeting both Mya and Lucas as well. While she didn't hug Mya, she did hug Lucas. "Hey, big brother. About time you got here."

Stunned, Mya glanced back and forth between the two until Scarlett laughed, reaching up to pat Mya on the shoulder. "I can see my grandson has been doing a good job of holding out on you. Come; let's go get better acquainted."

Scarlett slipped her arm around Mya's and led her out of the room and down the hall, Lucas and April bringing up the rear.

The foursome took an elevator to an on-site dining hall. Mya couldn't believe this was an actual long-term care facility. They were handed menus, servers waited on them, and a man was playing soft music on a piano from the corner of the room.

Sitting with Lucas on one side of her, Scarlett on the other, she spread butter on a roll, watching the butter melt as she moved the spread over the warm dough. She felt out of place, slightly blindsided, and could feel her walls starting to climb around her body.

Lucas sensed her struggle and reached out to give her leg a gentle squeeze as Scarlett spoke. "It's nice to see my grandson smiling so much. Are you the one responsible for this?"

Mya flushed, and again, sensing her hesitancy, Lucas once again took the lead. "She absolutely is."

He turned to fully face Mya, and she thought she saw sorrow in his eyes. "I knew if I told you that I was bringing you to meet my grandmother and officially meet April as my sister, that you would have done anything to stop it from happening."

April laughed across the table. "Mya, I know he can be intense. Blink twice if he is holding you against your will."

Lucas retaliated by wadding up a napkin, lightly tossing it at his sister.

"Children, knock it off!" Scarlett commanded the table, and with her few words, the two quickly sat up a bit taller.

The elderly woman took Mya's hand in hers. "My dear, I'm sorry that my grandchildren are acting like wild animals. I assure you it is not behavior I condone."

Mya's mouth ticked up into a smile. She thought she could really grow to like this sleek, classy woman.

"I've already met your parents; I thought it was only fair you got to meet my family, too." Lucas smiled at Mya. "My grandmother was married to Winston. The very Winston the flower shop is named after. Our mother and father," he gestured between himself and April, "were not present in our lives. We spent the majority of our adolescent years in different foster care homes and never even met Grandma Scarlett until about twelve years ago. It was hard at first, but we built a relationship, and now…well, now I have a family, and April and I have a family business."

Mya looked between the three others at the table. Scarlett's eyes were misty with unshed tears, April had a wistful look on her face, and Lucas just looked at Mya with a quiet apprehension in his eyes.

Never one to claim herself to be emotional, Mya knew she lived up to the ice queen reputation many thought her to have. But in that moment, as she sat at the table with Lucas, his sister, and his grandmother, she found herself becoming emotional, too.

Her heart panged for the fractured relationship she had with her own parents. She hurt for the lack of close relationships she had in her own life. But, at the exact same time, she felt hope that love and admiration could still be out there for her and that it would one day be celebrated the way the people at the table with her were celebrating each other now.

Under the table, she slid her hand into Lucas's, giving him a small squeeze. Looking around the table once more, she turned to him and gave him a small smile before turning back to Scarlett. "I am sure your reunion is a beautiful story, and I would absolutely love to hear more about it."

Chapter Nineteen

The Night of a Million Stars gala was less than five days away, and Lucas had completely thrown himself into his work as the night quickly approached. He texted Mya throughout the day, still took her on the two required dates throughout the week, but found that he increasingly missed her when they were not together.

Surprisingly, Mya found herself missing him, too.

She had grown accustomed to the way his palm felt in hers as they explored the city together, the way the weight of his arm felt as he casually slung it across the back of her shoulders while they were cozily tucked into hidden back booths, how his exquisitely soft lips tasted as they skated over hers, always a silent promise for more, as they made out like sex-crazed teenagers in a dark corner of a school dance.

Mya had become consistent about leaving work on time over the last few weeks, determined to better separate her work and personal time. As she had done for the last week, she sent Lucas a quick text as she exited the building that housed the interior design firm where she worked. A recent uptick in crime in the area of the building had Lucas's protective side flaring, and he insisted she sent him a text when she left the building as well as when she arrived home.

His protectiveness didn't feel overbearing; in fact, it felt fiercely genuine, and Mya relished in the feeling that he cared enough about her to be concerned for her safety.

***Mya:* Made it home safe and sound.**

Lucas: Good girl, Sunflower. Thanks for letting me know.

***Mya:* You're welcome. How long will you be working tonight?**

***Lucas:* Last shipment needed for the gala was just delivered about an hour ago. It's going to be a long night.**

Hurrying to her room, Mya shimmied out of her pencil skirt and into yoga pants. She pulled an over-sized tee over her head, pushed the hair out of her face with a chunky headband, and slipped her feet into a pair of sandals.

Grabbing her bag, she was almost back out of her apartment when she paused, turning to grab one of the paintings she had recently finished. Mya searched the kitchen for a grocery tote, finding a few haphazardly tucked under the kitchen sink. Shaking one out, hoping to release some of the wrinkles from the canvas bag, she slid the painting carefully into the bag for protection before leaving her apartment.

Less than an hour later, Mya stood in the doorway of the back door of the flower shop, quietly watching Lucas work for a minute before lightly rapping on the doorframe to gain his attention. She had the tote and her purse slung on one shoulder, a giant paper bag being held by flimsy handles in her other.

Lucas turned at the sound, his clear blue eyes staring at her in surprise.

Mya's belly did a small flip-flop as she stared back into the icy blue pools of his eyes. She adored his eyes and the expansive range of emotion that swirled behind them. Some days they were dark, so dark they were almost black. A chill ran over her body when she thought back on the times she had seen his eyes that color-always when they were being intimate,always when he was in control. Her mind wandered, thinking of how many other women had made his eyes take on such darkness, but she quickly pushed the thought from her head.

Other days, Lucas's eyes were clear and light, almost icy in appearance. But Mya knew that while his eyes appeared icy, that those were the times he was content and happy. She saw his eyes take on that love and happiness when he was with his family, when he talked about Winston's Flowers, and when he was volunteering and spreading joy to others. Seeing him like that, when he was light and full of life, was when she loved him most.

An imaginary vice tightened around her heart at the word.

Love.

Did she love Lucas?

Mya didn't have time to continue to mull over her thoughts as Lucas came to stand in front of her. He took her bags, setting them on a nearby counter before lightly kissing her. "What are you doing here, beautiful?"

He ran a finger over her velvet headband. "I like this…like seeing more of your face."

A wide grin spread across Mya's face as it often did with his compliments. "Thought you could use dinner. I brought enough in case April was here, too."

Almost as if Mya had conjured the woman by mentioning her name, April entered the backroom, her eyes fixed on the overflowing stacks of merchandise in her arms. "The front is all locked up, the register is settled, and everything's wiped down. I can run to grab us food so we don't die of starvation tonight."

Only after April set down the precariously stacked merchandise did she look to her brother and Mya who still stood only inches apart. "Oh, Mya! I didn't know you were coming by tonight. Did you come to help?"

Bashfully, Mya looked to April. "I'm afraid I'm of little help when it comes to the amazing things you both do, but I *did* bring dinner."

April's eyes brightened in response. "I could kiss you, Mya!"

Lucas scoffed. "That's my job."

"Down, boy," April responded to her brother with a laugh.

The trio continued to make light conversation as Lucas grabbed a small folding table from a nearby storage closet and started to lay out the assortment of to-go containers Mya had purchased from a local Chinese restaurant. The break couldn't have come at a better time for the siblings who had been working on fumes through much of the day.

Paper plates and plastic cutlery in hand, they all loaded plates full of spring rolls, lo mein, orange chicken, and steamed vegetables. Grabbing stools that usually flanked the large center worktable, the trio ate with plates in their laps. Mya laughed at stories Lucas and April shared of their time working together. She loved the glimpse into Lucas's life, loved seeing the love he shared with his sister.

After they cleaned up the remnants of their meal, April excused herself to head upstairs to Lucas's apartment for a quick shower leaving Lucas and Mya alone. During their meal, April explained that she commuted to the shop from Brooklyn and that instead of traveling back and forth each day, she was staying on Lucas's couch until after the gala since they were working more hours than usual leading up to the event.

"You know," Mya offered once it was just her and Lucas, "staying on a couch for multiple nights cannot be that comfortable for your sister. I do have a guest room she is more than welcome to use for the next few days."

Lucas brought his arms around Mya, and she craned her head up to meet his eyes. "You wouldn't mind that?"

Mya replied with a noncommittal shrug of her shoulders. "Why would I? She's your sister. You love her and I lo…eh, well, I guess I kind of like you."

Capturing her lips with his, he grinned into their kiss, speaking while their lips still touched. "Well, I guess it's a good thing that I kinda like you, too."

Truthfully, he didn't just kinda like the woman.

Lucas was full-on head-over-heels in love with her. He knew she loved him, too. Hell, she had all but confessed it just a few moments ago before diverting her words to less intense feelings. He wasn't going to push her to say it yet, and he sure as hell wasn't going to scare her away by admitting his feelings. But in that moment, with her wrapped in his arms, he knew this was exactly how he wanted to spend the rest of his life.

Making to move, Lucas tightened his arms around Mya, unwilling to let her go just yet. "What if April stayed here, and I stayed at your place?"

Confusion spread across Mya's face when she looked at him. "Why would you want to sleep in my guest room when you could stay in your own bed?"

A wolfish grin spread across his face. "I was kinda thinking I could stay in your bed. With you."

Lucas reached into his back pocket, withdrawing his wallet. Opening the well worn bi-fold wallet, he took out a small, folded piece of paper that Mya immediately noticed was the menu from Happy Endings. Unfolding the paper to reveal Mya's hand-written agreement, he pointed to number four on the list. "It says no sexual intercouse. It doesn't say I can't lay in bed with my arms wrapped around you all night long."

Her face drew into a look of skepticism. "Do you really think that is a good idea?"

"I only think it's the best idea I've ever had."

She took the paper menu from between his fingers, staring at it with bewilderment. "I can't believe you kept this."

He laughed as he took it back from Mya, folded it, and placed it back inside his wallet for safekeeping. Throwing a wink at Mya, he said, "I thought it would be kinda cool to show our grandkids one day."

Mya's cheeks flushed pink while heat crept slowly across them. Momentarily, her mind wandered to what life would look like with Lucas. Would they have children? Did he even want children? He had been joking about having grandkids one day, right?

A few seconds later, April reentered the back room, fresh from her shower in an oversized tee and boxer shorts, distracting Mya's mind from further drifting.

Lucas locked eyes with Mya but spoke to his sister. "Slight change of plans, April. You're gonna stay in my room until the gala is over; I'm gonna crash at Mya's."

He noticed a small flash of defiance in her glare, but Mya resisted pushing back against Lucas, knowing his mind was already made up. Besides, if she was being honest with herself, she was looking forward to having that strong, broad chest pressed up against her as she slept.

While Mya had planned to enjoy dinner with Lucas and then retreat back to her apartment, she found herself unable to leave. Instead, she spent several hours with Lucas and April, helping out wherever she could with small tasks like trimming stems and transporting flowers between the multiple refrigerators.

As she stepped to the back counter to bring a vase to the center of the room, her eye caught the canvas grocery tote sitting atop the counter. "Oh, I almost forgot; I brought you something."

She returned to the table with the vase and tote in hand. Mya was confident in her ability to paint. Although it was a recently revived part of her, she found her technique was still sharp, and as cliché as it sounded, it really was just like riding a bicycle. However, she still held her breath as Lucas slid the canvas from the bag and brought it up to eye level to admire.

Lucas's eyes went wide as he took in the singular large sunflower staring back at him. Against a background of muted browns, it eclipsed almost the entire canvas. Hundreds upon hundreds of individual petals flanked the center where even more detailed seeds created a deep brown center. No two petals were the same, some perfect while others showed flaws. And while it was clearly a painting, Lucas could have sworn that if he brushed his fingers over the canvas that it would feel just as smooth and velvety as the real thing.

His eyes darted between the canvas and Mya's face

several times. Unable to pull himself away from the work of art in front of him, he spoke almost to the canvas, turning to her at the last possible second. "Mya, baby, this is…stunning."

"Do you really think so?"

April glanced around Lucas, angling to get a glimpse at what had her brother in awe. Eyes going wide and mouth dropping to a small "o" shope, she turned to look at Mya. "You painted that?"

Mya coyly nodded.

"Stunning doesn't even begin to describe it, Mya. That's *magnificent*! Have you ever thought about selling your artwork? I mean, if you don't already?"

Lucas tore his eyes from the canvas once again in time to see the look of silent longing on Mya's face. He knew how important her art was to her, knew that she never had the support to pursue it further while she was growing up.

A small, noncommittal shrug heaved from Mya's shoulders. "I would love to. Someday."

The younger woman seemed to contemplate Mya's response for a minute before continuing, "You should partner with us."

Mya tried to speak, but April cut her off. "I'm serious! We could display several of your pieces up front along with the flowers, and then we could offer custom paintings as an add-on to our services. Imagine a bride being able to hold onto the memory of her wedding day with a one-of-a-kind painting depicting her wedding bouquet."

April was full-on squealing, giddy with the idea, and Lucas felt his heart momentarily surge as he looked back and forth between two of the most important women in his life. "That's actually a really good idea. I'd love to see what else you've done, maybe bring in a few pieces on a trial basis."

Flashing Lucas a small grin, Mya spoke with a sense of pride laced with hope. "Well, then, I guess it is a good thing you are staying at my place for the next few nights."

Yes, Lucas thought to himself, a very good thing indeed.

Chapter Twenty

Although it was nearly midnight when Lucas and Mya stumbled through the elevator doors to the penthouse, Mya was just as eager to show her paintings to Lucas as he was to see them. Dropping his overnight bag onto the couch, he strode towards Mya's makeshift art studio she had set up in the corner of the penthouse but stopped to take in his surroundings. His first time back inside the apartment since they signed their new arrangement, everything was the same, and yet everything was different.

Lucas noticed that there was sheet music atop the piano, a blanket sat unfolded on one end of the sectional, and there was a glass sitting half full on the coffee table-no coaster in sight.

She had increasingly seemed to relax over the past few weeks and now, looking around the place, he saw that extended to her personal space as well as her demeanor. Lucas didn't want to dig too deeply into that, but he hoped at least part of that change had to do with him.

"Come on beautiful woman, show me the goods."

Suddenly self-conscious, Mya slowly made her way to where Lucas was standing. Taking his hand, they crossed the room together, coming to a stop in front of the easel. She reached up to turn on a small light that was affixed to the contraption and began rifling through a small cabinet she had been keeping her finished pieces in.

Mya lined two smaller paintings up on the edge of the easel, handed a third to Lucas, and turned two additional paintings towards him as she held them in her hands.

Eyes darting between the paintings, Lucas couldn't decide where to land his gaze first. Each piece was more beautiful than the last. Swirling colors danced across the canvases, creating stunning realistic-looking flowers and landscapes. Some were views Lucas recognized-Central Park and the Flatiron building-while others were simply gorgeous florals against solid backgrounds.

"Baby…" Lucas's low voice trailed off.

Setting the painting down from his hands, he took the two from Mya next, making sure to place them down on the floor with extreme caution. He took Mya's face between his hands, tilting her face to meet his stare. Lucas's eyes darted back and forth between hers. Gingerly, he captured his lips with his. "You're so fucking talented."

Sighing against his lips, Mya responded, "I was afraid you wouldn't like them."

"Are you fucking serious? I want all five of these for the shop and more if you have them."

Nodding, she slid her hands around his waist, loving how his strong back felt under her hands. "You can have anything you want."

A deep chuckle rumbled from Lucas. "Oh, sweet girl, how are you gonna tempt me like that?"

Ignoring him, she pulled away. "Come on; we both have to be up early. Let's get some sleep."

Lucas was already in bed when Mya slid between her sheets. Men had it so easy, she thought, simply brushing their teeth and *maybe* washing the day off their faces. Meanwhile, she had brushed and flossed her teeth and washed, toned, and moisturized her face to the high heavens before plucking a few stray hairs that sprouted between her brows. She brushed her hair, applied a moisturizing lip balm, slathered lotion over her skin, and only then did she tug on a pair of sleep shorts and a matching tank top.

She wasn't in the bed for more than ten seconds before Lucas pulled her close. Chest to chest, Mya noticed he only wore a pair of boxer briefs. Instinctively, her hands came out to rest against his muscle as one of his large hands gently ran through her hair.

"Mmmm, this feels nice." Lucas was surprised when the words left his own lips, but he couldn't deny that it did feel nice. He had never been a cuddler. Hell, until Mya, he had never taken such care while planning dates and rarely made it to a second date. But something about her had captivated his mind and body from the very first time he laid eyes on her. He wanted to keep her in this bed, tangled in his arms forever.

The scent of her minty toothpaste caressed his face and tickled his nose as she let out a long sigh. "It does feel nice."

"Mya..."

Briefly, she shook her head. "Don't, Lucas. Just... just hold me, and let's close our eyes."

Lucas gave her a nod before pulling her closer, brushing a kiss against her lips. "Sleep well, Sunflower."

Her eyes were already closed as she responded, a small smile on her face as she drifted off to sleep.

Waking in the middle of the night, Mya made a quick trip to the bathroom before returning to bed, already feeling more rested after a few hours of sleep than she could ever remember feeling. A gentle glow of moonlight bathed the bedroom in a low light, and Mya's eyes skimmed over Lucas's body in silent appreciation. The sheet had been pushed down, fully exposing his chest, and he was sprawled out on his back, one arm bent behind his head with the other resting on his stomach. Her eyes drifted even further down his body, and her lips parted when she saw the way his penis had tented the sheet that was slung low on his hips. Suddenly, her mouth watered with need, and her nipples pebbled under the thin satin fabric of her sleep tank.

Lucas gently snored as she continued to stare at him. She wanted to touch him, wanted to feel his hands on her skin as she had weeks before. Their relationship was new and fresh, but she couldn't remember a time in her life before Lucas when she felt so appreciated and cared for.

She had written the terms of their arrangement, and Lucas had accepted them without hesitation. Mya knew that bullet point number four was hard for him—no sexual intercourse. She saw the way he looked at her longingly over the last few weeks, felt the way he kissed her and caressed her skin, heard the need in his voice when they spoke.

And she was feeling it now, too.

Before she knew what she was doing, her body moved of its own accord. She lightly pushed the sheet the rest of the way to the edge of the bed and climbed on top of Lucas. Her body clenched as she felt the familiar length of his cock brush against her pajama-clad core, the wetness quickly building between her thighs. Leaning over his body, she kissed him on the lips before whispering into his ear, "Lucas"

When he didn't stir, she increased the volume of her voice slightly, trying again. "Lucas, wake up."

His eyes shot open, and he looked to her with sleep-filled confusion in his deep blue eyes. Lucas brought his hands to Mya's arms, concern lacing his voice. "Baby, what's wrong?"

"Nothing." It came out a breathless whisper. She rocked against him once, twice, three times. "I want to amend the arrangement."

His dick hardened further under her hips and as he pushed himself up on his forearms, Lucas was aware that he was suddenly fully awake. Though he wanted to-damn did he want to-Lucas refrained from putting his hands all over her body. "Is this your idea of a joke, to wake me up in the middle of the damn night, sitting on top of me in that slinky silk top and shorts, wiggling your hips over my cock? Because if this is a joke, Mya, it's just fucking cruel."

"No. No joke. I...I want you. I don't want to wait anymore."

"Baby, you need to tell me exactly what you want from me. I'll give you everything you fucking want, but I will not have you coming back to me later, telling me that I broke our arrangement."

Brazenly, Mya slid her hands up her body, cupping her breasts in her hands before lightly pinching her own nipples through the light fabric of her tank. She had never felt so powerful as she did in that moment. An incredibly sexy man under her, giving her the power to make the rules. "I won't. I wouldn't. Just... touch me, Lucas. Please."

Without warning, Lucas pulled Mya down to his face. He kissed her deeply, their mouths parting, making way for their tongues to explore one another as she moaned into his kiss.

Lucas slid a hand up the back of her neck and into her hair, forcefully wrapping his fingers through her silken black tresses. Pulling her face away from his, he growled. "Tell me where you want me to touch you, Mya."

"My breasts. Touch my breasts."

Obliging her request, he trailed both hands up her stomach until they came to palm her tits. He groaned as the tight little buds of her nipples stiffened even further under the careful ministrations of his fingers.

Needing to get even closer to her, he only stopped to pull her tank over her head, immediately returning attention to her chest.

"What else, baby?"

Her chest heaved as she leaned into his touch. "I want to feel your mouth on my nipples."

God damn, he wanted this woman so bad.

Without hesitation, he flipped them over, Mya now laying with her back to the bed. He left a bruising kiss against her lips then moved to her neck before trailing kissing down her chest. Lucas licked slow, tortuous circles around her nipples, showering each breast with attention. He pressed her tits together, traveling back and forth between her nipples as his cock throbbed against the heat radiating from her tight shorts.

Mya groaned, her hands coming up to tangle in Lucas's hair.

"Use your words, baby girl." He nipped at her breast, and she yelped against the fleeting pain that coursed through her body in response.

"Taste me, Lucas."

"Where?"

A momentary shyness crept over Mya, but she pushed it aside. "I want you to pull my shorts down and taste me there."

"Say it. Taste you where, Mya?"

"Between my legs. I want you to lick me between my legs."

"You want me to lick your pussy, don't you?" Lucas forced a hand between their bodies, dragging his fingers over the flimsy fabric of her shorts. He could feel the dampness that was pooling against the fabric and how wet she was for him. Fuck, it turned him on, but before he would relent and taste her sweet cunt, he was determined to get the prim and proper Mya to talk dirty to him.

"Yes."

"Tell me. I need to hear you say it."

"Lucas," she whimpered as he continued to tease her through her shorts, "I want to feel your mouth between my legs. Lick my pussy, please."

At her words, his primal need kicked in. He was feral, climbing off her only long enough to shimmy her shorts from her body, he brought them to his nose, inhaling her scent before tossing them to the ground. "God damnit, baby, do you know how good your cunt smells?"

Mya's body flushed under his words. She had never been one for dirty talk, but Lucas knew exactly what to say to make her body vibrate with need. And she wanted more of his words, of his praise and quiet affirmations spoken only when the two of them were alone and naked.

Lowering his head to the apex of her thighs, Lucas placed a kiss to the top of her sex. Hands coming to rest on her thighs, he pushed her legs further apart before nuzzling her folds with his nose. Parting her pink folds with one hand, the other stayed locked on her thigh, fingers digging into her skin. With one fluid motion, he licked up the length of her pussy before settling his lips over her already sensitive clit.

"Ohhh." Mya purred the word, arching her back off the mattress and bringing her hips closer to the luscious lips that devoured her. "That feels so good."

"That's right, baby. Let me make you feel good." His response was muffled against her skin, unwilling to break away from her pussy. "You taste fucking exquisite, Mya."

Sliding two fingers deep inside, Lucas relished the tightness as her walls gripped his digits. He lavished her clit with sloppy, wet kisses, licks, and tiny nips as she squirmed against the mattress and his face.

"Harder," she panted. "More."

Obliging her request, he added a third finger, watching in awe as her pussy stretched to accommodate his fingers. She was so fucking beautiful, her juices coating his fingers and sliding down his wrist, making it easier for him to thrust deeper and harder. He imagined how she would look with his entire fist in her cunt, and the thought caused his already strained cock to throb almost painfully. "One day, baby, one day I'm going to slide my entire fucking fist inside you and fuck you with it until you cum."

With those words, he dropped his head back to her clit, wrapping his lips around the most sensitive place on this woman of his dreams. He sucked on her, applying tantalizing pressure that sent her body into convulsions as she came undone.

She was cumming. Hard. Her body bucked off the mattress, a sheen of sweat glistening over her belly as her hoarse moans filled the otherwise silent room.

Tearing his lips from her body, Lucas growled at her. "That's a beautiful fucking girl, Mya. But I'm not done with you yet. I'm not gonna be done with you until you soak my face with your juices."

With that, he pulled his fingers from her cunt, liquid trailing out from her pussy. Lucas slapped her cunt-hard. Mya screamed into the abyss of the room but before her scream was finished, Lucas was back between her legs with his tongue, licking and sucking. He lapped at her cunt like a kitten after a saucer of milk, coating himself in her delicious taste.

One hand still on her thigh, the other came to her clit, and he pinched the bundle of nerves between her legs, sending Mya into another fit of ecstasy. She swore she saw spots as she came, her body shaking as Lucas continued to lick and suck along her overly sensitive pussy.

Her hands came to tangle in his hair, and he trailed kisses over her sex-swollen pussy lips and gorgeous thighs. He loved her thighs almost as much as he loved seeing her splayed out, writhing under his tongue.

With one final long and tortuous lick, he pushed himself up to his knees, wiping the back of his hand over the bottom half of his face as he looked down on the woman under him, a salacious grin splayed across his still damp lips.

Wanting to take in the beautiful sight of Mya, he allowed his eyes to trail over her naked body. Nipples still in tight little peaks, her chest heaved as she tried to control her breathing. Perfectly sculpted shoulders trailed upwards into a gorgeously long neck reminiscent of classically trained ballerinas. Lucas knew he could get lost in worshiping her body for hours-days even.

Their eyes met, and long seconds of silence stretched between the pair. It was Lucas who spoke first, softly as if not to distract from the energy buzzing around them. "You'll never know how beautiful you are when you are stretched out for me, Mya. It's the most glorious view in the entire fucking world."

Leaning over her, Lucas brought himself to the bed while supporting his weight on either side of her body.

He wanted, no-he *needed* to taste her lips. Lightly, he licked the seam of her lips before gently taking her lower lip between his teeth. As he bit, he growled his approval. "I'm gonna be a very tired man in the morning Sunflower, and I'm not gonna care one fucking iota."

Unabashedly, Mya lifted her hips from the bed enough to feel his cock press against her. "Then we better make it worth the lack of sleep for both of us."

"Oh, sweet girl, it has already been worth it for me."

It had been worth it for Mya, too, but she wanted more, wanted to give Lucas the sweet release he had already given her…twice.

As his lips came to rest against hers, she spoke, "So you're saying you don't want to fuck me tonight?"

"No, baby. I want to fuck you every night." He kissed her lips.

"I want to fuck you every day." He kissed her deliciously long neck, trailing his tongue down the sensitive flesh where her neck and shoulder met.

"I want to fuck you in the sun and when the rain pours down outside our windows. I want to fuck you first thing in the morning when I open my eyes and and at night right before I fall asleep."

He ground his hips against hers. "I want to spend every second of the rest of my life inside your beautiful, tight pussy. I want to sear the memory into my mind so it's what I remember as I take my last fucking breath on this earth."

Reaching between herself and Lucas, she ran her hand over the length of his cotton-clad boxer briefs. "Then let's start right now."

Lucas didn't need to be told twice. In one swift movement, he climbed off the bed and pulled his briefs down his thick thighs. Mya stared at his body in appreciation but was cut short as he grabbed her ankles and pulled her to the edge of the bed. "Get on your knees for me, baby. Get on your knees and spread that pussy nice and wide for my cock."

Damnit, this man had a way of making her drip with words alone. Clamoring into position, goosebumps spread across her flesh as Lucas ran a large hand down the length of her spine. He trailed his hand over her ass, over the tight puckered skin of her tight asshole, and between her legs. "God damnit, you're so responsive. So wet."

"For you, Lucas. It's all for you."

He pumped his cock with his hand, several long and languid strokes. "Fuck, I have to grab a condom."

Without hesitation, Mya looked over her shoulder and spoke. "No. You don't."

Frozen in place, his eyes darted between the cock in his hands, the glistening pussy on display in front of him, and her gorgeous hazel eyes staring back at him.

"I'm on the pill."

Lucas couldn't remember the last time he had sex without a condom. Hell, he didn't think he ever had. It was too intimate, too close to telling someone that you fully loved and trusted them without using words. But he wanted to give that to Mya, wanted to tell her that he loved her and would cherish her forever, even if he couldn't say it with words yet.

"I'm clean." They were the only words he could muster up the courage to say.

She smiled, a small, coquettish grin across her kiss-swollen lips. "I trust you, *Sir*."

A rumble erupted from deep within as he settled himself against her entrance. Momentarily, he teased her cunt, sliding it against her clit, through her folds. And then, with one deep thrust, he filled her with his dick.

Mya winced against the short burst of pain as he became fully seated inside her body. Giving her a moment to adjust to his size, he trailed light fingertips over her back. "Fucking beautiful, Mya. You're so fucking beautiful."

She whimpered in response, slowly moving her hips while trying to acclimate to his size. God, she felt so full, a delicious stinging stretch that overtook her entire body.

Achingly slow, Lucas began to pump in and out of her pussy, bringing himself almost completely outside of her body before sliding back in. There was no doubt in his mind that this woman was made for him, from the way her body stretched to accommodate his cock to the way she rocked back against him, silently begging for more. The way she flushed under his praise to the way she drove him fucking bat-shit crazy, Mya was the woman for him. He wanted to wife her up, pump her full of cum until she was carrying his baby, and grow old wandering the streets of New York City with her hand in his.

Jesus Christ, where had those thoughts come from?

Pushing those thoughts aside, he refocused on the moment he was in, sliding in and out of Mya, picking up speed until he was like a mechanical piston, thrusting into her with brute force. Sweat beaded on his brow, droplets falling from his skin.

Reaching beneath Mya, he grabbed her breast, kneading the flesh and toying with her nipple. Giving it a small tug, she gasped, arching her back further into the air. He lived for her sounds, her gasps and moans, the silent pleadings for more when she was close to orgasm.

"Baby, do you trust me?"

"Yes, Lucas. Always." She was gasping for air as she spoke, looking to fill her lungs with the sweet sex-tainted air that swirled around them, their unique scents blending together, melding into one.

A firm hand landed in the middle of her shoulder blades. "Lean forward, Mya. Lean forward for me."

Doing as he requested, she leaned down until her chest was flush with the mattress under them, her arms resting at either side of her body.

One strong hand landed against her ass, an audible echo bouncing around the room. Lucas looked down to see a blooming handprint taking shape where his palm had landed, and it caused a smile to spread across his face. God, she was fucking perfect.

Deep inside her, Lucas stilled, loving the way her pussy clenched his dick. He was pretty sure he could cum just like this, her tight walls milking his cock for all it was worth. But he wasn't done with Mya yet.

One hand on each asscheek, he spread her wide, looking at the beautiful, untouched hole staring back at him. Bending to get closer, he opened his mouth, letting a trail of saliva fall from his lips onto her asshole.

"Lucas?" Her voice was laced with trepidation.

With one hand still on her ass, the other slipped between them, spreading the moisture of his spit over her most forbidden hole. "Relax, baby."

He continued to circle her ass as he began pumping into her cunt again. "Relax and let me do the work."

Bringing his hand to his mouth, he spit into his palm before returning it to her puckered hole. Letting the saliva fall onto her, he used his thumb to gently spread more of his spit. Massaging her, releasing the tension building in her body, he slowly pushed his thumb into her ass, stopping at the first sign of resistance. It was almost immediate.

"Baby, I know it's tight and uncomfortable, but you're going to feel so good with both your tight little holes filled."

She took in several shallow gasps. "I…I don't think I can."

Lucas wasn't having it. "Yes, you can. Come on; deep breath in, baby girl."

Mya wanted to please him. She wanted to give in to all the sensations Lucas made her body feel. She did trust him explicitly, and until he did something to break that trust, she was going to believe he really did have her best interest at hand.

With her body trembling, she took in a long, deep breath through her nose and held it in.

"Good girl. Now, let it out slowly."

She did, and as she exhaled, he pushed his thumb deeper inside her. Repeating the process, she inhaled and exhaled, and each time she did, he pushed deeper, past the rings of muscle clenching around his thumb.

God, he wanted to fuck her in her tight little ass. But she was nowhere near ready for that. Yet.

With his dick sheathed in her pussy, thumb up her ass, he leaned over her back, relishing in the feel. "I'm going to move now."

Words eluded her; a small nod against the bedsheet was all she could manage. She felt stretched and full-oh so full. What would his dick feel like back there in the place his thumb currently was? She shuddered at the thought as Lucas slowly began to move.

Keeping his hand still, he focused on thrusting in and out of her wet sex. The sound of flesh slapping against flesh filled the room along with the delicious squelch of Lucas's dick invading her cunt. "God damnit, Mya, you sound so beautiful when you take me-the sounds your body makes, the sounds *you* make."

Fists clenching in bedsheets, she gripped, trying to find purchase as Lucas slammed into her over and over and over again. "Close-I'm so close."

Lucas's thumb slid in and out of her ass, gaining speed as he continually pistoned his hips. "Yes, baby, yes you are. Cum for me, Mya. Cum all over my cock."

Pumping into her one, two, three more times, she came undone as he thrust harder and deeper. He pulled his thumb from her ass, smacking her over the handprint that still marred her flawless skin.

She lay on the bed, sated and spent as he continued to assault her cunt with his dick, chasing his own release. He snaked a hand beneath her, holding the full weight of her limp body up with one strong arm. "You want me to stop, I'll stop, but right now all I want is to cum inside your tight little pussy."

"No," she found strength, pushing herself up so her back was flush against his chest, her arm reaching up to wrap around his neck. "I want you to cum inside me, Lucas. Claim me. Make me yours."

Fuck.

He roared, increasing speed as he thrust into her. "I'm gonna paint the inside of your pussy with my cum, baby. But let's get one thing straight; you're already mine. You've been mine since the first fucking day I saw you across that church. It might have taken two years, but you've always been fucking mine, Mya."

"Yes, Lucas. Yes, Sir. Yours. Always yours."

Hearing her confirm his words sent Lucas careening over the edge. The tension that had been building at the base of his spine exploded, and he came inside Mya with long, hard thrusts. Hot seed coated her walls, his balls pulsing as more and more and more spilled into her body.

They stilled, bodies locked together before dropping into a heap of limbs on the mattress. Mya turned to face Lucas, and he pulled her closer, kissing her lips as the telltale signs of his release slowly leaked out onto her thighs and the mattress beneath them.

Long, unhurried kisses passed between them, fingers trailing over each other's bodies. Lucas brushed Mya's hair behind her ear, placing another kiss on her lips.

"Baby."

Her response wasn't coherent, a garbled mess of consonants and vowels melding together.

"Look at me."

Mya brought sleepy eyes back to Lucas as he spoke.

"You may be mine-in some way you always have been; I wasn't lying to you about that. But make no mistake, Mya, I'm just as much yours as you are mine. And if you let me, I'll spend every fucking day making you understand that. You just need to be willing to dive into the deep end with me, because if you do, I promise I will worship you every fucking day, mind *and* body. So, what do you say? Jump into that deep end with me, Mya? Be mine, and let me be yours."

While still clouded by sleep, her eyes were clearer now, emotion swirling in the hazel depths. Mya searched between his eyes, searching for something, anything, that would tell her this was a terrible idea. But she found nothing other than want and need and desire, the same feelings swirling through her own body whenever it came to Lucas Gentry.

Gently reaching out, she traced her fingers over his lips, leaning in to press hers against his while nodding against him.

"Okay. Let's jump into the deep end. Together."

Chapter Twenty-One

MYA HEARD Lucas call out for her across the penthouse as she stood in the bathroom, placing the final touches on her look for the gala. She had given him an elevator key a few days earlier, making it easier for him to come and go from her apartment while April remained at his place overlooking the flower shop.

Although Lucas had spent the majority of the day at the hotel setting up for the event, he insisted on picking up Mya from her house, arriving at the event together.

Making her way through her home, she entered the foyer, coming to stand in front of Lucas who was in a slim-fitted black tux. She spun in a small circle, a smile over her perfectly painted red lips. "What do you think?"

"Baby," he crooned, feeling almost as if he was floating high above in space, looking back at the earth and all its glory for the first time. Stepping closer to her, he placed a kiss on her cheek before taking her hand and holding her at arm's length. "You look fucking spectacular."

Mya wore a dark, pine green ball gown that looked like it had been custom designed to her body. The halter top left little to the imagination, the slope of her breasts on full display. A thick sash of the same green fabric circled her waist before falling to the ground in a full A-line. Every inch of the gown, sans the sash, was covered in what looked like thousands of crystals, making her shimmer and shine whenever light hit her silhouette. The back, or lack thereof, was equally as stunning. Aside from the fabric holding up the halter, there was nothing shielding her skin. Cut all the way to right above the top of her ass, Lucas couldn't wait to rest his hand on the exposed small of her back as often as he could throughout the night.

There was no way she was wearing a bra with that dress and the thought of that made Lucas's mouth go dry.

"If we don't leave in the next thirty seconds, we're

never going to make it out of here without me tearing that dress from your body."

Mya laughed, grabbed a small clutch from the entryway table, and pressed the button to call the elevator. "You're such a caveman sometimes."

As they rode to the ground floor, Mya took a pair of earrings from her clutch, affixing the dangling diamonds to her ears.

"Oh, speaking of jewelry," Lucas pulled a long, thin blue box from the inside pocket of his tux jacket and handed it to Mya with the little wink she was quickly coming to love. "Just a little something to remember the night by."

She knew it was Tiffany & Co. from the box alone. The signature Tiffany blue staring back at her from her slightly trembling hands. Tentatively, she opened the box to find a sparkling platinum and diamond tennis bracelet. It was simple enough to wear daily, but elegant enough to complement her dress with small round and oval diamonds interspersed between one another. A bracelet like this must have cost him *thousands*, she thought.

It was too much, and as she was opening her mouth to protest, the elevator doors opened and Lucas ushered her out to the lobby of her building. Taking the bracelet from its box, he looked at Mya. "May I?"

Any protest fell off her lips, and she nodded,

looking at the beautiful man in front of her, affixing the equally beautiful bracelet to her wrist with deft precision.

"It's stunning, Lucas-so beautiful. Thank you, I love it."

He tucked the box back into his pocket before wrapping an arm around her bare back. "You deserve only the most beautiful things, Mya-the most beautiful things for the most beautiful woman in the world."

Exiting the building, Lucas ushered Mya towards a waiting limo, surprise once again etching her features as the driver exited the vehicle to open the door for the couple.

"Mr. Gentry. Good evening, Ms. Monroe," The older gentleman greeted them as Lucas helped Mya to slide into the vehicle, climbing in behind her and taking the spot right next to her in the oversized car.

Taking two glasses from the built-in cabinet, Lucas popped open a bottle of champagne, filling the glasses before handing one to Mya. Holding his glass up to hers, he spoke softly, "To tonight, to tomorrow, to all the days we'll spend together."

They clinked glasses, each taking long sips from their respective glasses. Lucas set his glass down before running light fingers up and down Mya's forearm. He could sense the tension in her body. "What's wrong,

Sunflower?" He trailed his fingers over the bracelet around her wrist. "Do you not like it?"

"No! I love it; I really do." She let out a long sigh. "I guess I'm just nervous about tonight."

He raised an eyebrow at her, prompting her to speak without using words.

"This is the first time I'm going to see a lot of the people who were supposed to be at the wedding. My parents are going to be there. Dave will probably be there with his family. It's just nerves."

Mya had spoken with her mom several times over the last few weeks and while the woman had stopped acting like her daughter and Dave would be reuniting, she did little to stop her distaste for Lucas from being known. It was a new point of contention between the mother and daughter and just one aspect of what was increasing the nerves swirling through Mya's body.

Leaning into her, Lucas took her hand in his, linking their fingers together. His voice was laced with sincerity and a hint of vulnerability he often hid. "Does any of this have to do with being with me, with accompanying me to the gala tonight?"

Visibly confused, Mya shook her head. "What? Lucas, no."

"Mya, I know I'm so far outside of your social circle that I'm basically in a different orbit. I'm not an overly rich businessman who travels the world making multi-million dollar deals. I don't have a trust fund or grand plans for my life. I'm just a simple florist. I know you deserve someone so much more than me and that I might be selfish for trying to keep you, but God dammit, Mya, I promise to cherish you and keep you safe every day that you'll let me."

His vulnerability was crushing her.

Without thinking, Mya crawled on top of him, one leg on either side of his body with layers and layers of fabric cascading around them. She placed one hand on either side of her face, cradling him as she gazed into his stunning blue eyes.

"Baby," she whispered, and it wasn't lost on Lucas that it was the first time she ever called him anything other than his name outside of the bedroom.

Mya closed the inches between their lips, crushing hers against his in a fierce, almost punishing kiss. She didn't care that she was probably smearing her lipstick all over her face, didn't care that there was someone mere feet away with only a small tinted partition between them. She simply needed to show him how right he was for her.

Pulling away, her chest heaved, mimicking the movement of Lucas's own chest. "I deserve you, and you deserve me. I promise you that what I am feeling is just the culmination of weeks of fallout from the wedding. I also promise you that there is no one else on Earth that I would rather be with tonight than you."

Leaning back in, she kissed him gently again. "We're in the deep end together, remember?"

He pulled her into his chest, wrapping his arms around her bare back, just holding her there for long, silent minutes as they inhaled and exhaled together as one.

Finally separating from one another, Mya used her thumb to wipe stary lipstick from Lucas's lips before ungracefully climbing off his lap.

Their moment had been sweet and intimate-vulnerable on both of their parts-but of course, it didn't stop Lucas from growing increasingly hard with Mya on his lap. The layers of fabric from Mya's dress shielded her from feeling him pressing against her, but she couldn't help but notice him trying to rearrange himself in his pants as the limo continued to drive towards the event, giggling at his attempts to hide the impressive bulge straining against the fitted pants of his tux.

"Told you that you were a caveman."

He shook his head at her, laughing. "Watch it, Sunflower. A real caveman would drag you over here and fuck you before we ever even made it to the gala."

Feigning shock, she reached over Lucas, purposely grazing his still straining cock, pressing a small button built into the wall. "Excuse me, sir, would you be able to provide us with an estimated time of arrival?"

The driver's voice crackled over a speaker, "Traffic is a bit congested ahead, ma'am, but we should be arriving in about twenty minutes."

Mya sat back in her seat, taking several sips of her neglected champagne. "Twenty minutes. Whatever will we do to pass the time?"

Before Lucas could respond, she was on the floor of the limo, spreading his legs apart and reaching for the buttons on his tux. Mya brushed the jacket apart before moving her hands to his pants, unzipping and unbuttoning them before running her hands over Lucas's brief-covered cock.

"Mya, you don't have to." He leaned forward just enough to place a gentle finger under her chin, tipping her face up to his.

She didn't break eye contact as she responded. Instead, continued to tease him mercilessly over his boxers. "I would never do anything I didn't want to do. You have helped me to learn to stand up for myself. You make me feel sexy. I want to, Lucas. Let me take care of you the way you take care of me. Let me make you feel as good as you make me feel."

Lucas pushed her hands away, pulling his cock from his briefs, and jerking himself with long strokes from root to tip. With his other hand, he cradled her face before tracing her plump, perfect bottom lip with his thumb, smearing her perfectly painted lips.

"You do make me feel good, Mya. Your pleasure is my ultimate pleasure. Feeling your wetness around my cock is the most amazing feeling in the world, and while I crave your mouth on me, right now I want nothing more than to feel your cunt pulse around my cock as you come undone on top of me. I want you so full of my cum that it drips down your thighs when you walk into that gala with me tonight, so full of me that anytime you have an ounce of sadness or regret, you feel me between your legs and forget about anything and everything that isn't me. So, get off that filthy floor, climb up here on my lap, and be just as filthy on my dick."

She loved when he spoke to her like such a filthy woman. It made her thighs even slicker with desire, and with Lucas's help and constant praise, she was beginning to understand that there was nothing wrong with feeling sexy at such filthy words. If anything, it was empowering.

Eyes blazing with desire, she pushed off the floor of the limo, taking care not to hit her head on the roof of the vehicle.

"Take off your panties."

Doing as she was told, she shimmied her panties down her legs before placing them in Lucas's outstretched hand. He groaned when he felt the wetness that had already soaked through the thin, black lace.

Mya fought with layers of fabric until she was situated across Lucas's lap once again. Her hips came up enough for Lucas to reach between them, pushing his pants down enough for his cock to fill the space between their bodies. Guiding his cock to her entrance, he didn't dive into her, didn't even gently sink his length into her waiting sex. Instead, he held himself completely still at her opening, letting the gentle movement of the limo rock his cock back and forth against her clit.

"Please," she whimpered.

"I'm not stopping you, baby. I'm right here. Take what you want from me and show me how good it feels when I'm inside of you."

Not wasting time, she lowered herself fully onto his cock and slowly started grinding her hips back and forth. Tentatively, Mya rode him, her arms holding onto Lucas's shoulders for balance. He hissed in response, his own arousal heightened by the small moans slipping from her rosy red lips.

Taking her arms from his shoulders, he reached upwards, placing her palms on the roof of the limo. He teased her skin with his fingers, trailing them down the dangerously low-cut front of her gown. "This gown is beautiful, but I can't help but think it will look even better in a heap of frilly fabric on the ground."

Shock flitted across her features. "You wouldn't dare."

He lay back against the seat, pulling his lip between his teeth as he watched her work herself up and down, down and up. "You don't wanna tempt me, Mya."

She dropped a hand from the ceiling, but Lucas immediately replaced it. "I love watching you fuck my cock, baby, but if we have any chance of finishing before we get there, I'm gonna have to speed things up a little."

Without waiting for her response, he brought them to the edge of the seat while she still sat on his cock. Winding a strong arm around her body, he nipped at the skin on her neck. "Hold on, baby."

Relentlessly, he pounded into her body. Over and over, he thrust while keeping a tight hold around her waist. Mya's hands slipped along the upholstered roof of the limo as she tried to steady herself. Arms extended, she pushed harder against the ceiling with each thrust of Lucas's hips.

He was doing the work, but sweat still broke out across her skin and trickled down her exposed spine. She was sure her hair was a mess, that her makeup had run, and that her dress had wrinkles throughout the luxurious fabric. But she didn't care. She was a mess-she was *his* mess. And he liked her just as much when she was smeared and squirming on top of his cock as he did when she was perfectly put together.

Mya didn't know if Lucas was capable of love, if he would ever tell her that he loved her, but in this moment, she felt it. And for the first time in her life, she felt ready to give her full love in return. In all its messy, complicated glory.

"God, Lucas. You make me feel *alive*."

"You are alive, baby. So fucking alive, Mya."

He tightened his grip on her, his free hand coming to rest around her neck as they held each other's gaze, a clash of hazel and blue eyes mixing together, reflecting the need they shared between them.

Leaning into his hand, Mya forced him to apply more pressure. "I'm not afraid anymore, Lucas. Take me over the edge, Sir."

Fucking hell.

Lucas exploded. He squeezed the sides of her neck, and Mya gasped for air as his hips hit piston speed. Over and over and over and over, he pounded into her, the sounds of their bodies filling the quiet air around them.

She wasn't in her body anymore.

Mya was floating over them, watching herself in slow motion, and she let herself go and allowed this man to love her in his own special way.

"So close…Lucas…I'm…I'm going to cum." Her voice was strained and hushed from the restriction of air to her lungs.

Groaning as his own release neared, his gruff voice filled the back of the limousine. "Do it, baby. Soak me."

With his final word, he released his grasp on her throat, and she screamed, a guttural scream from deep within her stomach, as her orgasm racked her body. Stars dotted her vision as Lucas found his own release, pulsing deep within her pussy.

He held her body, still and sated against his while his cock continued to twitch deep within. "You're fucking everything, Mya. Everything."

Contentment radiated from her body. She truly felt like everything to him in that moment.

"Lucas."

"Hmmm?"

"Why did we stop moving?"

And quickly, the moment melted away as she hurried to straighten herself before stepping out of the limousine with Lucas on her arm.

Chapter Twenty-Two

A LOW DIN of noise filled the ballroom as Lucas and Mya made their way into the event space arm in arm. All around, people conversed and laughed, drank and danced. Despite the crowd, Mya didn't see anyone as all her attention was turned to the transformed space.

She hadn't seen the ballroom before the transformation took place but had spent enough time at event spaces over the years to know how much effort went into taking a blank box of a hotel ballroom room and turning it into something truly magnificent. Mya had seen some truly abhorrent decorating over the years, but with the Night of a Million Stars gala being one of the biggest fundraising events of the year, it was no surprise that the hotel ballroom had been truly transformed just as it had in years past.

Everywhere she looked, the room had morphed to fit the Alice In Wonderland theme the invitations had alluded to. Mya had seen what Lucas had been working on for the night, so she knew what to expect, but seeing the space in person stole the breath from her lungs.

Humongous crystal chandeliers hung from the ceiling, flanked by gorgeous draping silks in bright jewel tones. Large round tables filled the space, radiating out from the central wooden dance floor and stage. Each table's centerpiece varied, some large and grand while others instead had several smaller pieces grouped together for an overall cohesive feel.

Flowers pouring from antique teapots, a photo spot with a spectacular fresh red rose backdrop, and decor incorporating vintage clocks, birdcages, and hats filled the space. The entire room was low lit by thousands upon thousands of small, fairy-like lights, sending the room into an almost constant shimmer. On the stage, a live band played, and numerous guests were dancing to the upbeat sounds.

Honest to goodness shrubs lined the perimeter of the room, various flowers peeking out from their greenery, and out the corner of her eye, Mya spotted a larger-than-life teacup like the ones she only remembered seeing on a long ago family trip to Disney.

Everything was bright and colorful, whimsical and fun, yet sleek and upscale. Mya felt like she had truly been transported to a magical realm outside of New York City, and she stared in awe at not only the room, but the man next to her that helped to make it happen.

When she finally spoke after what felt like a lifetime of taking in the event, her voice was breathy. "This is…I don't even have words, Lucas."

He flashed her a grin in return, one of those rare, vulnerable, yet devilish grins she loved so much. "I guess it'll do."

She playfully smacked his chest, and he responded in mock hurt.

"I'm serious. It's magical. Beautiful. Magnificent…"

Lucas pulled Mya into his arms, pressing his lips to hers. "You're very good with listing adjectives that describe yourself, baby."

She blushed, and he slid a hand to her lower back, ready to escort her to their table.

"Mya!" The woman's voice was familiar to Mya; and she stiffened against Lucas in response before turning to face her now ex-best friend.

Before she could make introductions, Charlene threw her arms around Mya. "Babe, it is *so* good to see you! I'm so sorry about what happened between us; I truly am. But I've missed you *so* fucking much!"

The woman turned to look at Lucas, not trying to hide the way her gaze appreciatively grazed his body. She bit her lip, pink lipstick staining her bright white teeth, her expensive perfume hanging in the air heavy around them. "And who do we have here?"

Flicking his eyes between the two women, Lucas could sense Mya shutting down, the walls she worked so hard to tear down being rebuilt in front of his eyes. It pained him to see her crawl back into the shell of the woman she had been before he met her, yet he wasn't sure how to bring her back from the brink.

Extending a hand to the woman, he introduced himself as Mya submissively stood at his side, almost frozen in fear at the sight of the woman. "Lucas Gentry-pleasure."

Charlene gasped. "*The* Lucas Gentry? I've seen your work-very impressive. No wonder our girl Mya here has seemed to take a liking to you. It appears that you are just as gorgeous as your floral displays." The woman ran a hand up his forearm to his bicep. "Truly a pleasure to meet you. Now, if you'll excuse me, I'm sure my fiancé is around here somewhere. Toodles!"

She waved her hand in a dismissive flick of her wrist and disappeared as quickly as she arrived, but not before Mya could make out the ring on her left ring finger.

Mya's engagement ring-the same one she had worn during her engagement to Dave.

Trying to propel herself forward but failing, she stood firmly rooted to her spot on the floor while people continued to mill around them, fluttering from place to place within the walls of the ballroom. Her eyes welled with tears, and she quickly blinked, trying to stifle the inevitable fall.

"Mya, look at me." Lucas's voice was firm, bringing her back to the present. She snapped her neck, tilting her chin until she could look into his blue eyes, those eyes that grounded her and steadied her, just as much as his strong arms did as they wrapped around her in a crushing hug. "Come on."

Without waiting for her to move, Lucas pulled her toward a wall of shrubbery. Pushing open a panel from the wall, he tugged her into what appeared to be a small janitorial closet. "Listen to me; you get five minutes right now to fall apart over this."

The tears had already started to fall as she looked at him, lip quivering. "Wh…what?"

It nearly killed him to see her like this.

"Five minutes to be upset. To be mad or sad or whatever it is you're feeling. Then, we're walking back out to that gala."

"You and me-" he gestured between their close bodies, "we're gonna drink, we're gonna dance, and spend a shit-ton of money winning overpriced charity auction items that we don't fucking need. We're gonna enjoy the night, not let that horrible excuse for a woman bother us, and we're gonna have fucking fun."

Reaching into the pocket inside his tux, Lucas attempted to pull out a cloth handkerchief. Bringing his hand up to Mya, he did a double take, stopping himself when he realized he was about to wipe her tears with her lacy panties he refused to give back to her before they stepped out of the limo.

She caught sight of his clenched fist, saw the flimsy material peeking out from between his large fingers, and stifled a small laugh.

Lucas found the fabric square he had been looking for and swiped it across Mya's delicate features, drying the tears that had streaked her face. She was still as he held the fabric to her nose. "Blow."

"Ew." She took the handkerchief from his hands. "There are a lot of things I've been willing to let you do to me, but I draw the line at you blowing my nose for me."

Mya blew her nose before tucking the soiled fabric into her small clutch.

"Baby, it's not me doing something to you; it's me doing something *with* you."

She reached up, threading her arms around his neck. "I suppose you're right."

Lucas ran his fingers through her hair, not caring if he messed it up. "I could get used to you saying that I'm right."

Mya let out a sigh. "Lucas?"

He continued twirling her tresses through his fingers. "Mmm?"

The tears were back as she spoke, soaking the fabric of his tux as he continued to hold her close. "Am I really so hard to love? My parents, Dave-hell, even my own best friend. I just…I just want to be loved."

Full-on sobs wracked her body.

He wished like hell that he could absorb her pain.

Lucas sat on a nearby overturned five-gallon bucket, cradling Mya on his lap. "My sweet, sweet Sunflower. You *are* loved. Your parents-they're not used to showing their feelings, but I would put money on the fact that they love you with every fiber of their being, even if they haven't shown it in ways that make sense. You have your Charlotte; I know she loves you. I knew it from the day she showed up looking for you at the shop after I blindsided you at the bar. The woman threatened to cut my balls off if I ever hurt you."

That got a small laugh from Mya.

Lucas continued, "April loves you. She adores having you around the shop and looks up to you. Hell, my grandmother certainly loves you. She already wants us to have great-grandchildren for her."

They sat in silence for a few minutes, Lucas not pressing her to return to the gala happening just a few feet away.

Suddenly, Mya's voice was almost a whisper. "Lucas?"

"Yes, baby?" His response was equally as hushed.

"Could you ever love me?"

"I already do, baby."

The words left his mouth, shocking him and Mya equally.

He hadn't expected to admit that to Mya so freely. Lucas had always guarded his heart, tarnished by foster families that tossed him aside. He always wanted to find love and was fortunate to find his family, but he never expected he would find a woman like Mya who showed him love through her actions, even when she felt anything but loved herself. He cherished her, felt for her what he had never allowed himself to feel for any woman before. And he didn't want to hide the love that was coursing through his veins.

She peeled her body away from his enough to peer up into his eyes. Lucas's face was soft, his eyes swirling with emotion.

"There isn't a thing I don't love about you, Mya. I love watching you blossom into the strong, confident woman you are becoming. I love your heart, your ability to give to others more than you would ever take for yourself. And even more, I love the man you have helped me to be. You make me believe that I am worthy of love, too, ya know."

Mya smiled up at him before placing her head back against his chest, that strong, broad chest that was her favorite place to lay her head.

And while the words were still but a whisper on her lips, she stunned Lucas by admitting something from deep within her soul.

"I love you, too."

"I know you do, baby. You have shown me every day since I crashed brunch with your family at Tavern On The Green, since you gave me a chance. Since you gave me a piece of your beautiful soul and gorgeous body."

The duo sat on the overturned bucket for several minutes, way past Lucas's self-imposed five-minute time limit, as the sounds of the gala seeped in from the small crack around the doorframe. They were silent, no words needed to be spoken, as they held onto each other, full of silent promise words couldn't convey.

Finally, Lucas nudged her from his lap, helping her to smooth the wrinkles that had set in over the length of her gown.

"Come on, Sunflower. Let's go show these fools how to have a good time."

Chapter Twenty-Three

GALA IN FULL SWING, Mya was finally able to start enjoying herself. It might have had something to do with the third glass of champagne she was currently sipping, but she had a sneaking suspicion it had much more to do with the beautiful man at her side.

The beautiful man that she *loved*.

"There is my girl," Mya's father's voice commanded the room, much as it always did, as her parents came to stand next to the pair who were up next at one of the elaborately- themed photo ops that had been staged around the room. This one was a full tablescape made to look like the Mad Hatter's tea party.

For the first time in as long as she could remember,

she welcomed her parents with open arms, giving them both hugs as she made the decision to work through her own past to learn to accept them as they were. "Mom, Dad, you remember Lucas."

The two pairs sat at a nearby table, conversing lightly while watching everyone around them enjoy the evening. Mya's astonishment flooded her features when her mother complimented Lucas on his work for the event and she swore she saw the slightest blush creep up his cheeks under the woman's praise. Her mother was not one to dole out compliments lightly, and after their brief interaction, she was sure Lucas was aware of that fact.

"Thank you, Mrs. Monroe. As a former foster child, this event is of particular importance to me. While I never have been afforded the honor of attending in the past, I was honored when they reached out to me to help with the event."

On stage, the musicians began a slow and sultry rendition of "Stay With Me," the smooth sounds of the singer's voice filling the air. Lucas looked to Mya with longing before turning his attention back to her parents. "If you'll excuse us for a moment, I have yet to dance with your stunning daughter tonight. Would you do me the honor, Mya?"

Placing her palm into his outstretched hand, she let herself be led to the dance floor. Among the top tier of

New York City's rich and famous, Lucas expected to feel left out, like an outsider who didn't belong. Instead, at Mya's side, he felt a quiet sense of peace wash over him as he held Mya close and swayed to the melodies. They were two broken souls from very different lives who found love in the arms of one another, and as they continued to dance, he ran his fingers lightly up and down Mya's back, her skin rippling with anticipation at his touch."

The song came to an end, a second slow ballad picking up where the previous had stopped. Mya, still in Lucas's arms, looked over to see her parents swaying together, a rare smile on each of their faces as they laughed at a joke only the two of them seemed to hear. She couldn't remember ever seeing either of her parents look so at ease with one another, although she supposed she hadn't often given much thought to their relationship. For the first time, she realized she may have been wrong about the lack of love they had for one another.

Mya scanned the memories swirling through her brain as she swayed slowly side-to-side in Lucas's arms. Family vacations, social events, and high-pressured benefits accounted for much of her life. But the more she thought back, she remembered the smaller moments-her mom cooking her father his favorite meal for his birthday each year, the two working together to finish the Sunday crossword puzzle. Suddenly, she knew without doubt that they did care for one another and that perhaps, they simply had a hard time showing it when in the presence of others.

As the second song ended, the couples were side by side, Mya's father speaking in his ever-commanding tone. "Mr. Gentry, think I could steal my daughter from you for a dance?"

"Only if I can steal your lovely wife for a dance of my own."

Switching partners, Mya admired watching Lucas make his way around the dancefloor with her mother on his arm. At first, both Lucas and her mom appeared tense, but as they continued to move around the room, she noticed they settled into an easy routine as they chatted with one another. They appeared to be enjoying each other's company, a rare smile tugging at her mother's lips. She loved watching the pair laugh, seeing the familiar crinkle in the corner of Lucas's eyes. When he caught her looking from across the floor, he shot her a wink as he tipped her mother back in a mock dip.

Chuckling from her own dance partner brought her back to the present. "He's quite the charmer, Mya."

"Yeah, I suppose he is."

"I owe you an apology."

Mya looked at him, a small crease of confusion forming between her brows that was just barely visible beneath the fringe of her bangs. "What do you mean?"

"Your mother and I-we weren't always fair to you growing up. We pushed you into what we wanted for you without any regard for what you actually wanted, for what you actually deserved. I can't help but think that if it wasn't for us pushing you towards what we wanted, that you never would have gotten hurt by Dave. You would have made your own friends instead of being pushed into friendships with people like Charlene. After Lucas joined us at brunch, your mother and I had a long talk. We want you to be happy, Mya, and while it may take time for your mother and I to fully trust Lucas, we want to be there for you- with *all* your decisions. I'm truly sorry, Mya. For everything. "

Trying to speak, Mya could feel the emotion bubbling up in her tight chest. "It's okay, Daddy."

She couldn't remember the last time she had called her father "Daddy." Easily ten years. But at that moment, hearing his confession in the form of an apology, it felt necessary.

Her father was trying to rebuild the bridge that had so long ago been severed between them. The least she could do was reciprocate.

Mr. Monroe gestured towards Lucas and his wife, a soft smile capturing his face, weathered by years of hard work, late nights, and stress. "Does he treat you right?"

Mya met her father's gaze as he turned back to her, a soft smile on her own lips and a longing in her hazel eyes. "More than right. The very first day I met him, he asked me what I wanted-not what anyone else wanted or what anyone else wanted for me, what *I* wanted for me. He's inspired me to start painting again and even hung a few of my paintings in his shop." She was gushing, and tears pooled in her eyes, but she simply couldn't stop. "He's kind and generous, fiercely protective of his family, fiercely protective of me. It's new and exciting, yet at the same time, he feels like home to me."

Pulling his daughter in close, he wrapped her in a hug as the song reached an end. "That's all that really matters, then, isn't it? I'm proud of you, Mya-proud of you for charting your own course. I'm only sorry I didn't push you to do it from the start."

Mya smiled up at her father through mist-filled eyes as her mother and Lucas rejoined them.

Speaking from the stage, the emcee of the event urged everyone to return to their seats, giving a five-minute warning before bidding would start on the items up for auction. Aside from the cost of entrance to the gala, this auction was where the majority of their fundraising happened.

Lucas and Mya walked toward the table first, her parents idling around, speaking to long-standing friends and business associates.

"Your mom and I had a nice chat out there." Lucas motioned back to the dancefloor.

"Believe it or not, so did my dad and I. He apologized for not always being there for me or supporting me. He feels partially to blame for pushing me into a relationship with Dave."

"Same with your mom. She apologized to me for treating me brashly and asked if I would give her a second chance. She does love you, Mya."

They locked fingers as they neared the bar, their last stop before the bidding began.

Returning to the table, fresh drinks in hand, Lucas leaned into Mya, speaking so only she could hear. "What are we going for, baby?"

"Why are you whispering?"

"I don't want anyone to hear what we're going for and try to take it from us."

Mya threw her head back, laughing. "Very competitive of you, Mr. Gentry."

"Oh no, you don't!"

Before Mya could protest, Lucas had scooped her up and deposited her onto his lap. Wrapping his arms around her waist, he nuzzled into her neck, tickling her with his beard and nipping lightly at her skin. "What's my name, Mya?"

"Lucas! It's Lucas!"

"And what should you never call me?"

Thankful the chatter in the room hid her squeals, she tried- and failed- to escape Lucas's strong grip. "Mr. Gentry! Never Mr. Gentry, always Lucas!"

He pulled her even closer, kissing her cheek. "You're my good girl, aren't you, Mya?"

Feeling sassy, Mya decided it was her turn to be playful. Dropping her voice an octave lower than normal, she rasped into Lucas's ear, "I think you much prefer when I'm a bad girl, *Sir*."

She added the sir at the last moment before pulling away, retaking her place in the seat next to him as her parents rejoined them at the table.

Lucas wanted to haul her out of the ballroom and devour her right then and there, but he settled on shifting in his seat, trying to stifle his growing erection at hearing his girl speak to him with such defiance. Maybe he really was a glutton for punishment.

The emcee droned on, auctioning off designer handbags, jewelry, spa treatments, and more. No one at the table had bid on anything, mostly spending their time conversing with each other and gently joking about the many people bidding on the auction items.

"Next up," the emcee said, "an all-inclusive weeklong stay at the most romantic resort the Maldives has to offer. The winner's stay includes round-trip first-class airfare for two, a private bungalow over the water, a private chef, couples spa treatment, and many more exclusive perks. Bidding will begin at $12,000."

A squeal echoed throughout the ballroom, and when the heads at their table turned, they saw it was none other than Charlene. The woman looked eager to win the trip, holding a paddle up with a number showing her bidder's number.

Quickly, the vacation reached $20,000, and it seemed as if Charlene was going to win her trip.

Lucas looked at Mya who seemed to have zoned out, not paying attention to her former best friend. Instead, she sat closer to her mom, chatting with the woman as they only half paid attention to the auction.

"Going once," the emcee boomed across the room.

Flicking his gaze between Mya and Charlene, his mind was made up.

"Going twice!"

He was taking his girl to the fucking Maldives.

"$21,000." Lucas raised his hand into the air, showing off the paddle assigned to him.

Mya and her mother immediately stopped talking, her father joining in the look of stunned faces staring at him.

"$22,000!" Charlene called out.

"\$23,000," Lucas spoke nonchalantly before Charlene even finished increasing her bid.

"\$25,000." The woman looked at him, venom in her eyes as she held her paddle high in the air.

"\$30,000."

Charlene started to lift her paddle, but her hand was pulled back by a man Lucas recognized as Dave. His face was set in an unreadable neutral appearance, but Lucas could see the man silently seething. He was unaware if it was due to him pulling Charlene's apparent dream vacation out from under her or if it was due to Charlene so brazenly spending his money without consequence. Lucas didn't really care, so long as he won that vacation for Mya.

"Once," The emcee called, looking between Lucas and Charlene.

Lucas kept his gaze trained on Charlene, silently daring her to increase her bid.

"Twice."

Charlene tossed up her arms before storming out of the ballroom, Dave close behind.

"Sold to bidder 631! Thank you, Sir, the foundation will certainly be able to do amazing work with your donation."

Lucas sat at the table, a smug grin on his face.

"What the hell was that?" Mya continued to stare at him, dumbfounded by what had just taken place.

Shrugging his shoulders, he looked at her, mischief glinting in his blue eyes. "What? I've always wanted to go to the Maldives."

Across the table, Mya's father began laughing. He stood, coming to Lucas and clasping a firm hand on his shoulder. "Well, son, that is certainly one way to make a statement." Looking to his wife, he continued, "I think it's getting late for us older folks. What do you say we leave the kids to enjoy the rest of their night?"

Lucas and Mya stood, and while she hugged her mother, her father leaned into Lucas, patting him on the back as he spoke out of earshot of the women. "I failed her many times as a child and an adult, but she told me tonight that you have had quite the positive effect on her happiness. Take good care of her, Lucas."

Nodding at the man, he swapped places with Mya, welcoming the hug from her mother as Mya hugged her father.

"I meant what I said, Mya." Her father spoke close to her ear. "I am so very proud of you for everything. Your mother and I both are."

As they pulled apart, Mya overhead her mother speaking to Lucas.

"Again, I can only continue to apologize to you for my behavior. She is extremely important to us, and I can see now that she is equally as important to you."

As her parents walked away after promising to have

the pair over for dinner soon, Lucas slid his arms around Mya from behind, resting his chin on her shoulder. "So, you want to go on vacation with me?"

She laughed, leaning back into him. "Yes, but don't ever pull something like that again."

Lucas straightened, turning Mya to search her eyes for some semblance of emotion. "What do you mean?"

"I know you did that for me because you wanted to take something from her the way she took something from me. I appreciate everything you do for me, but I can fight my own battles."

"God, Mya, where did you come from?"

"I'm pretty sure they just left."

He barked out a laugh, hugging her like she might disappear if he let go. "Let's go, baby. I've gotta date with that smokin' hot green dress that I've been dying to rip off of you all night."

Epilogue

One Year Later

Waking with a yawn, Mya looked over at the sleeping giant next to her with a sleepy smile on her face. Lazy rays of early morning sun trickled in through the gauze-like curtains that separated their room from the turquoise blue waters of the Indian Ocean while the gentle lapping of the waters created a melody that lured Mya from the bed.

Wrapping a sheet loosely around her sun-kissed body, she walked the few steps to their private balcony that jutted over the sea, perching along the double-wide lounge chair that occupied most of the small outdoor space.

Today was their last full day in the Maldives, and Mya didn't know if she would ever be ready to leave such a magical place. Fairly certain Lucas would have to carry her back to New York City kicking and screaming, she momentarily played with the idea of handcuffing herself to the bungalow's balcony in protest.

They already had the handcuffs in their luggage that Charlotte playfully gifted them at their house-warming party prior to their departure and had made *very* good use of them over the last few days.

In fact, they had made good use of almost every surface in the bungalow during their stay.

The bed first thing in the morning and last thing at night.

The shower inside their room before an especially delicious meal served over the water.

The shower outside on their private wooden dock after a day of snorkeling among the coral reefs.

A smile curled on Mya's lips as she heard Lucas approaching from behind, his voice rough and heavy with sleep. "Morning, baby. What are you doing out here so early?"

She scooted forward, allowing Lucas to climb behind her. Falling back against his naked chest, she relished in the feel of his coarse beard against her smooth skin as he trailed his chin up and down the length of her neck. "Just thinking about how much I'm going to miss it here."

Grunting in agreement, Lucas ran his hands up and down her arms. "Maybe we can make it an annual tradition?"

"Depends on if you make any hasty decisions at the auction coming up."

After a small, shared laugh, the pair sat in near silence for several minutes, simply enjoying each other's company as birds cawed in the distance.

Lucas had been asked to once again head floral design for the upcoming gala, and they both knew that when they returned home, life would quickly kick into overdrive as final preparations were made.

Mya had left her job at the design firm a few months prior, and while she still didn't feel fully comfortable around the meticulous flower arrangements Lucas's skilled hands created, she had carved out her own path, painting to her heart's content and selling her artwork alongside the flowers at Winston's. Some of her work was even on display in hotels and condo lobbies throughout the city, thanks to the good working relationship she kept with her former employer.

Trailing his skilled fingers over her skin, Lucas deftly spread the sheet Mya had tucked around herself. She had blossomed in the past year, her confidence growing every day, her ability to ask for what she wanted coming easier to her now. No longer was she the woman who feared being left behind, and, in a way, Lucas's own fears of being cast aside diminished alongside Mya's.

Over the last year, the pair enjoyed almost weekly dinners with her parents, and a few times Lucas's sister and grandmother even joined. While Mya's relationship with her parents wasn't fully repaired, they had all put in the work and effort to grow closer.

Maneuvering her body to now face Lucas, she sat in front of him, fully bare and unashamed of her body.

He would never get sick of that sight, never get sick of finding new ways to make her moan and new ways to take control of her body.

Pulling her closer, he brought her up until she was straddling his lap, nothing between them but the flimsy cotton of his briefs. "The day is ours, baby. Any thoughts on how you want to spend it?"

The privacy of their surroundings made her bold as she rocked against Lucas, sliding her naked sex up and down the length of his already impressively hard cock, her breasts pressing against his chest. She loved that a year into their relationship, she could still elicit such a response from him, that he still craved her and worshiped her body every chance he could.

But it wasn't just her body that he worshiped; it was her mind, too.

And she reciprocated the sentiment, pushing Lucas

outside of his comfort zone just as much as he pushed Mya outside of hers. They continued their weekly deliveries to long-term care facilities, spreading joy to the residents, but more importantly, Mya had convinced Lucas to also start volunteering at the organization that hosted the gala each year. He had taken to his new role as mentor very seriously, dedicating time to three young men who were in the foster care system-the very system that failed Lucas as a child.

Together, they even talked about the possibility of becoming a foster family sometime down the road-way down the road.

For the time being, though, they were happy exploring life as a pair.

"Sunflower," Unaware she had drifted into a world of her own, his voice brought her back to the present, "where did you go?"

A sheepish little smile crept across her face. "I was just thinking."

He snaked his arms up her sides, playfully tickling her. "Spill it."

Batting him away, she settled back on the longue chair. "We've come a long way from the times that I kept trying to push you away."

He nodded his response. "You came to your senses though."

Laughing, she playfully pushed him away, but

Lucas used his strength to pull her close, kissing her fiercely and with all the passion that he held for her.

Abruptly, he stood from the lounge, making his way back into their bungalow.

"Where are you going?"

Ignoring Mya's question, Lucas grabbed his wallet and walked back to her. Sitting beside her, he opened his wallet and pulled out a small, folded piece of paper.

"I forgot I had something special for you." He handed her the paper and Mya immediately recognized it as a menu from Happy Endings, the dessert bar where they first wrote their arrangement.

"I can't believe you still have that," she said with a laugh.

"Open it."

Without hesitation, she opened it, expecting to see the arrangement they wrote just over a year earlier. Instead, across the top, this time in Lucas's handwriting, the words The Arrangement were written with only one bullet point listed under the heading.

1. Mya Monroe, will you marry me?

She read the simple sentence again and again, finally breaking contact with the menu to look at Lucas as he sat next to her, a single solitaire diamond ring delicately held between two fingers.

He sank to a knee in nothing but his briefs as Mya lurched her naked body into his arms, tears already falling.

"Tell me that's a yes, Mya. Please tell me that's a yes?"

"Of course, yes!"

He slipped the ring on her shaking hand, then held her close to his chest. Looking up to him, tears still in her eyes, she spoke softly, almost echoing her words from the first time they met at the flower shop. "Mr. Gentry, just maybe I *am* that kind of woman. Maybe happily ever afters are actually for me."

THE END

Acknowledgments

While writing has always been my passion, it wasn't until I was encouraged by my fiancé that I had the confidence to truly sit down and turn my thoughts into stories. With that being said, I must start by thanking her for being not only my biggest cheerleader, but also my inspiration, my first reader for each of my projects, my brainstorming buddy, and the person who can bring me back to Earth when I find myself spiraling out of orbit.

Next, to my amazing editor Tiffany from Tiff Writes Romance-thank you for always helping to polish my stories, for being an integral part of shaping me into a better author, and for always answering my questions between edits. I am so thankful to have you as part of my team!

Equally as important to the success of my work, a huge shout out to Tori Ellis from Cruel Ink Editing + Design. Without your eye for design, attention to detail, and crazy talent, my books would simply be words on a page. You help to turn them into works of art in both ebook and print form and I am forever grateful for the hard work you put into each book you format, truly treating it as if it were your own work.

To my awesome group of beta readers-with Natalie at the helm-thank you for always being there to test the waters, for pointing out major plot holes and inconsistencies, and for laughing alongside me when I'm panicking over quickly approaching deadlines.

Last, but certainly not least, to my amazing ARC readers-headed up by the wonderful team at KatieAndBreyPA. Thank you for your feedback, your reviews, and for your excitement over The Arrangement. Having you next to me, sharing in the ups and downs of publishing helps to make it all worthwhile!

About Amity!

Amity Malcom was born in Pennsylvania. She began writing short stories while still in elementary school-including a total page turner about how her mother loved to fish. Her mother does not love to fish and is actually terrified by ocean creatures.

She now resides in Florida with her fiancée, two completely insane but loveable cats and one neurotic but adorable dog.

When not writing steamy characters and happily ever afters, Amity can be found watching professional soccer, exploring Florida's many theme parks, and campaigning for LGBTQIA+ rights.

Other Works

Broken Sparrow
Collection:

INKED

HTTPS://TINYURL.COM/5N83NZ5K